Willful in Winter

The Wicked Winters Book Four

By
Scarlett Scott

Willful in Winter
The Wicked Winters Book Four

Published by Happily Ever After Books, LLC
Print Edition

ISBN: 978-1-672420-92-1

Edited by Grace Bradley
Cover Design by Wicked Smart Designs

For more information, contact author Scarlett Scott.
www.scarlettscottauthor.com

Rand, Viscount Aylesford, needs a fiancée, and he needs one now. His requirements are concise: she must not embarrass him, and she must understand he has no intention of ever marrying her.

Miss Grace Winter is the most stubborn of the notorious Wicked Winters. When her brother decrees she must marry well, she is every bit as determined to avoid becoming a nobleman's wife. She would *never* marry a lord, especially not one as arrogant and insufferable as Aylesford.

But pretending is another matter entirely. She has to admit the viscount's idea of a feigned betrothal between them would not be without its merits. Until Aylesford kisses her, and to her dismay, she *likes* it.

Soon, their mutually beneficial pretense blossoms into something far more dangerous to both their hearts…

Dedication

Dedicated to my wonderful editor. It's been a joy working with you all these years. Thank you for making each book the best it can be.

Chapter One

Oxfordshire, 1813

"WHILE YOUR OFFER is tempting, I must regretfully decline, my lord."

Surely Miss Grace Winter, undeniably the most stubborn chit Rand had ever met, had not just turned down his proposal. *No* female had ever turned down a proposal he had made.

Ever.

Granted, his proposals were ordinarily of a far seedier nature, and the females in question were demimondaines, but still.

He must have misheard her.

"I beg your pardon, Miss Winter," he said, frowning at her from where he stood in the Abingdon House library, "but I do believe I mistook your acceptance for a rejection."

She sighed, almost as if she found him tedious. "You did not mistake anything, Lord Aylesford. I told you no."

He frowned at her. "Women do not tell me no."

Miss Winter's lips twitched. "On the contrary, I stand before you as evidence they do."

Her lips were soft and full and the most maddening shade of pink. Every time he stared at them, he wondered if her nipples matched. But now, that mouth was laughing at him.

Laughing at his proposal.

Mocking him.

The daring of the chit was not to be borne. He ought to kiss her, he thought. Or turn her over his knee and spank her delectable rump. But he would do neither of those things. Because she was an innocent, virginal miss, decidedly not the sort of lady he preferred. And she was denying him.

"Why will you not agree to be my feigned betrothed?" he bit out.

"Because you are a rake," she said. "And one with an insufferable sense of his own consequence. If I am to be your betrothed, even your *feigned* betrothed, I will be required to spend time in your presence. To dance with you, to pretend as if I find your sallies amusing, that sort of nonsense. I would rather read a book, to be perfectly honest."

The devil.

She thought he was a rake.

Well, to be fair, he was. He had earned his reputation—that nothing in skirts was safe from him—the delicious way. He had bedded more women than he had bothered to count. The list of his conquests was longer than the Thames.

But she found him conceited? She did not want to dance with him?

"What is wrong with my sallies?" he demanded. "Why would you need to *pretend* to find them amusing?"

He was vastly amusing. All the ladies in his acquaintance told him so. They laughed at his every quip. Quite uproariously.

"I am making an assumption, of course," she said, waving a dismissive hand through the air, rather in the fashion of one chasing a bothersome fly. "I have never heard you tell one. But you do not look like the sort of gentleman who would tell clever sallies. You look like the sort who expects everyone around him to be easily wooed by his face and form."

Here, now. The baggage was not truly suggesting there was something amiss with his face? With his form? He engaged in sport whenever he could—riding, boxing, fencing, rowing. He was lean and tall. His muscles were well-honed from his exertions. And as for his face? Why, he was widely considered one of the most handsome men in London.

"I do not *expect* them to, Miss Winter," he informed her, his voice frosty with indignation for the series of insults she had paid him. "They *are* wooed by my face and form. With good reason."

She cast a dubious glance over him. "Your face and form are acceptable, I suppose. If one does not mind dark hair and blue eyes. I have always preferred blond hair and brown eyes, myself. There is something so delightful about the combination. And you are a bit thin, my lord. You might consider eating pie more often."

His face and form were *acceptable?* She was bamming him. She had to be.

He scowled at the impertinent chit, and in all his ire, he could only seem to manage one word. "Pie."

"Yes." She smiled sweetly. "Any pie you like. Consuming sweets ought to help you appear more substantial and far less gaunt, over time."

Rand had been careful to maintain a respectable distance between them for propriety's sake, even if the hour was late and there was nothing at all proper about arranging for a clandestine meeting with the unwed sister of his host. But he was not accustomed to doing anything the proper way. He was a scapegrace, it was true, and besides, everyone knew the rules of London eased at country house parties.

Did they not?

He decided they did. They had to. Especially when a man was as desperate as he was. And as irritated.

"Pie," he repeated, stalking toward her. "You recommend I eat pie, Miss Winter?"

She stiffened as he neared her, but she did not retreat, and nor did her goading smile fade. "I do, Lord Aylesford."

He stopped only when he was close enough for her gown to billow against his breeches. Her green eyes flared, and he noted the flecks of gray and gold in their vibrant depths. At this proximity, in the warm glow of the lone candle brace illuminating them, her auburn locks seemed as if they were aflame. And damn her, she was beautiful in an unconventional way. Tempting. Need roared to life inside him, sending an arrow of lust straight to his hardening cock.

"I am not hungry for pie," he told her softly.

And now, he was forgetting all the reasons he must maintain his distance. Forgetting he could not afford to compromise her if he wanted to remain free of the parson's mousetrap. Forgetting he wanted her to agree to become his feigned betrothed, and that none of this—the way he had been courting her at the house party, the way he felt now—was real.

Think of Tyre Abbey, he reminded himself. The wealthy Scottish estate would be his upon his betrothal, thanks to his grandmother, the dowager duchess' stipulation. He would convince Miss Winter to agree to his plan one way or another.

He had to.

"What are you hungry for then, my lord?" she returned, her gaze dipping to his lips.

His honed rake's instincts told him Miss Grace Winter was not as unaffected by him as she pretended. Not if the way her lips had parted, the sudden huskiness in her tone, and the manner in which she had swayed toward him just now were any indication.

Perhaps the means to convince her of the wisdom of his

plan was not words at all.

"You," he said, and then he drew her soft body against his.

Her hands came between them, twin shields uniting to keep him from his prize.

"I am not something which can be eaten," she argued mulishly.

He could not keep himself from grinning. "I beg to differ, my dear."

Oh, how delightfully innocent she was. Seducing a virgin was more entertaining than he had imagined it could be. Not that Rand was seducing her, mind you. He was merely inducing her to agree with him. To see the infinite wisdom of his flawless plan.

With the aid of his lips.

And perhaps tongue.

Her eyes narrowed and she gave him the most fetching scowl he had ever beheld. Most definitely with his tongue, he decided.

"I do not appreciate being laughed at, my lord," she snapped. "Perhaps you ought to rethink your strategy for wooing unwilling females."

"But surely you are not entirely unwilling," he countered, his grin deepening, for he knew this to be true. Every sign, aside from her bewitching scowl, told him she was attracted to him.

That, and the fact that he had yet to ever encounter a female who was not. He could not help it. He had been born to sin, with a face and form every woman loved.

"I am most certainly opposed to your farcical scheme and foolish attempts at kissing me both." Her lips pursed, as if she considered saying more, but forced herself to stop there.

Ah, amateur mistake.

She had revealed far too much.

"Who said I was going to kiss you, darling?" he asked, his grin subsiding as he stared deeply into her eyes.

They were the most riveting shade of green, he thought again. Deep and mysterious, like a dark, verdant forest.

She flushed. "You said…"

"Mmm?" One of her glossy auburn curls had slipped free of her coiffure, and he became mesmerized by it now. The hand on her waist slid slowly up her back, following the elegant line of her spine. The other brushed the curl from her cheek, his fingers lingering on her jaw. "What did I say?"

She did not shrug away from his touch, and he was thankful for it, because her skin was soft and warm and rich. She smelled of an English garden. A host of blossoms in summer. The sudden urge to taste the creamy flesh of her throat struck him. He had never been the sort to nibble on a lady's neck. But Grace Winter's neck was perfection. He did not think he had ever seen one finer. Just below her left ear, she bore a heart-shaped beauty mark that called for his lips.

Oh yes, he could consume her. For all that she was a virginal miss, she was utterly delectable. The notion of debauching her held more appeal than taking her as his feigned betrothed did in that moment. Which was saying a great deal, because Rand wanted Tyre Abbey, and he wanted it now.

"You said you were hungry…for *me*." The last word emerged from her as little more than a whisper.

"I never said I was going to kiss you," he countered.

She caught that luscious lower lip of hers between her teeth, revealing her uncertainty. "But you said I could be eaten."

Damnation, he was not prepared for the almost violent surge of lust her words produced in him. Was he so much of a rakehell that the notion of despoiling an innocent, of hearing her utter wicked things, made his prick go hard?

If she only knew what she was saying. What she was doing to him.

He cupped her cheek. "Do you know what I think, Grace Winter?"

She was worrying her lip once more, and he was jealous of those teeth. He wanted to nip that lip himself. "I did not give you leave to call me by my given name, Lord Aylesford."

No, she had not. And neither had she given him leave to take her in his arms or to touch her as he was now. But she had not pushed away from him or told him to stop, either. And her eyes had darkened. Her pupils were wide, obsidian discs. She was breathless. He knew enough about women to know when one wanted him, and this one most assuredly did.

Of course she did, said his rakish self-assurance. He had never wooed a woman who had not wanted him.

But still, there was a connection between them.

She felt it. He *knew* it. And now, she was going to pay for telling him he ought to eat pie, the minx.

"I think you *want* me to kiss you," he told her. "That is what I think."

GRACE STARED UP into Viscount Aylesford's unfairly handsome face. She had been having a great deal of fun at his expense. But somehow along the way, things had changed. She was flustered. Overheated. The fire in the library had not been banked properly by one of the domestics.

Or perhaps she had caught a lung infection and she was feverish.

Had she contracted some sort of nefarious ague?

Her mind stumbled over itself in an effort to find an explanation to the sensations coursing through her. All of them unwanted.

Think of the look of indignation on his beautiful face when you told him to eat pie, suggested Pragmatic Grace.

Let him kiss you, urged some inner devil she would not even lower herself to name.

That inner devil could *go* to the devil, as far as she was concerned, and it could take the rakehell before her with it.

He was looking at her, his expression almost triumphant. As if he had won. As if he had bested her. Of course, he had managed to rout her attack with his wicked brand of charm, and she had allowed him to gain the upper hand, even if momentarily. Oh, how insufferable the man was. Were all rakes this certain of themselves? This irritatingly lovely to look upon?

"I do not want you to kiss me," she snapped at him. "Unhand me, if you please. I have already told you I shall not be a part of your scheme to feign a betrothal between us."

"Grace," he said slowly. His thumb swiped over her lower lip.

The pad of his thumb, nothing more.

And she was aflame. That lone movement sent her crashing into a wall of heat. If her gown burst into searing licks of fire, she would not be at all surprised. What was it about this man's presence, his touch, that so undid her? Was it a rakish talent he had learned, or was it some wickedness he had been born with?

Dear heavens, what was wrong with her?

She broke herself free of his sensual spell and swatted at his hand as if he were an irritating bee buzzing about her on a lazy summer's day. The only trouble was, he was nothing at all like a bee, because she had never been entranced by such a creature. And she was drawn to the viscount in a way she ought not to be. She needed to gird herself against his silver tongue. Against his blinding masculinity.

Of course, such a man would be sure of himself. Doubtlessly, no woman had ever looked upon him and found fault. He was just that singularly glorious to behold. But he was also an arrogant oaf, and an aristocrat, and for that combination, she could not forgive him.

"Lord Aylesford," she said coolly, "I insist you conduct yourself with proper decorum."

"You insist, do you?" He grinned, and it was decidedly roguish.

Knowing.

She would have taken a step backward in retreat, but she was afraid it would seem a weakness to him. As if she could not stay within his hold and remain impervious.

When she could.

Her spine stiffened. "Yes, I insist. Your plot will not work, and nor will it come to fruition. You would do well to foist yourself upon some other unsuspecting lady at this house party. Surely, there are others who would do just as well."

"I am foisting myself on you, am I?" he asked, his grin disappearing.

Still, he did not release her.

And she wished his masculine scent of musk and amber and bay rum did not affect her quite so strongly.

"Can you doubt it?" she returned, her hands settling upon his upper arms.

A mistake, as it turned out, for they were well-formed. Muscled and strong. She *liked* the way they felt beneath her touch.

"I doubt it very much," he insisted. "If you were not interested, you would not have met me here in the library when I asked. Nor would you linger. Admit it. I tempt you."

His grin was back in place. Only, this time, it was not so much a grin as a taunting smirk.

"You do nothing of the sort." She attempted to fix her most fearsome frown upon her face. "As I said, you would be better served to find some other, far less intelligent and far more unfortunate female than I to play the role you seek, my lord. I have neither the time nor the desire to suffer your games."

"Prove me wrong, then," he dared her, his tone as provoking as his smirk. "Kiss me."

"Kiss you," she repeated, still clutching him as if he were saving her from plunging headlong over the edge of a cliff.

And perhaps, in a sense, he was.

"Yes." He raised a brow. "Kiss me and show me you are altogether unmoved. A veritable fortress. Kiss me and tell me then you are not tempted."

There was only one thing more foolish than agreeing to a clandestine meeting with a rakehell like Viscount Aylesford at a Christmas country house party. Only one thing madder than staying in his arms rather than fleeing.

That would be pressing her lips to his.

She stared at his mouth and swallowed, wondering—for the briefest of moments—what it would feel like against hers. Then she banished the unworthy curiosity. She had never been the Winter sister who longed for romance or swooned over men with wicked reputations. What was she doing here?

Run, said Pragmatic Grace.

But her pride would not allow her to go just yet, for the heated manner in which the viscount was looking upon her could not be missed. He expected her to kiss him and become so overwhelmed, she would agree to his madcap plan.

He was about to discover that Grace Winter was not to be

dallied with, and that in a battle of wills, she would always emerge the victor.

She rose on her toes and pressed a quick, chaste kiss to his cheek. And drat him for the slight bristle of his whiskers that sent heat coursing through her. And drat him doubly for the delicious scent of him, which she very much feared would follow her like a ghost.

Feigning a smile she did not feel, she disengaged from him. "There you are, my lord. You have had your kiss. As you can see, I remain utterly unmoved. Good evening."

Liar, taunted her inner devil.

Her heart seemed to thud with the resonance of it, faster now than ever. *Li-ar. Li-ar. Li-ar.*

She dipped into a frantic curtsy and did not bother to wait to hear his response before fleeing from the library and all the restless urges inside her that told her not to go.

Chapter Two

RAND WOKE WITH the devil of a headache.

And a dry mouth.

And an aching cock.

A deuce of a thing, to rise randy, yet still a trifle sotted from the night before. His temples throbbed. His tongue tasted of sour spirits. His ballocks were drawn tight with the need to find a willing woman. His hand idly stroked his shaft. Perhaps not any willing woman. Only one. The one who had turned him inside out in the library before telling him to go to the devil and fleeing.

Leaving him with blue ballocks and a prick hard enough to rival any marble statue's.

But he would not think of Miss Grace Winter now, he told himself.

No. To Hades with the stubborn chit. Instead, he would think of someone else. His eyes closed, shuttering the light of the country sun which was threatening the window dressings. Anyone else.

Yes.

Soft pink lips. Hungry pink nipples to match. Long, auburn hair he could uncoil from a chignon. Breasts that would fill his palms. Curvaceous thighs. A tempting heart-shaped mark on her throat…

Christ.

He released his cock and threw his head back into the pillow, exhaling on a harsh sigh.

He had been thinking of *her*. Imagining *her*.

His reaction to her was bemusing to say the least. She had kissed his cheek. His bloody *cheek*! And the unprecedented lust roaring through him at that lone, innocent buss of her lips had been enough to hold him in a stupor as he had watched her run from him in a swish of pale skirts.

The desire clawing through him had been so potent, in fact, that he had found his way into his host's brandy store. Hence this morning's headache. And dry mouth. And pervasive sense of self-loathing.

The raging lust, however, could not be explained.

He was not meant to desire Grace Winter. He was meant to use her to further his ambition of gaining Tyre Abbey. Indeed, he had chosen her because she had looked upon him as if he were an unavoidable mud puddle when he had been introduced to her. A lady who scorned him would suit his purposes well, he had thought, because she would not have any trouble crying off their feigned betrothal when the time came.

But somehow, along the way, he had forgotten his reason for choosing her altogether. Somehow, the need to convince her to agree to his scheme had been driven more by desire for her than by reason.

Pretending to be betrothed was meant to solve his problems, not create more.

His grandmother, the formidable dowager duchess, would not grant him Tyre Abbey until his betrothal was announced. Rand wanted Tyre Abbey. Rand did not want a wife. Hence, Rand needed Grace Winter.

Not to soothe the ache in his ballocks, he reminded himself.

Rather, to help him to gain what was rightfully his. And then break the betrothal so the two of them could go on to live their separate lives.

He had been obliged to attend this deuced Christmas country house party as an escort to his mother and sister. Making the best of his situation seemed wise. Attempting to get beneath the skirts of Grace Winter, however, decidedly did not.

Still, the notion would not leave him. There was no denying it. He was harder still, just lying here thinking about the damned impertinent bit of baggage. She had told him to eat pie. That his sallies would not be funny. That he should find someone else for his plan.

The trouble was, he did not want anyone else. He wanted Grace Winter, who was not easily won by his ordinary charm. On a sigh, he slid his hand back beneath the bedclothes once more. He told himself he had no choice. He could not carry on all day, playing parlor games and exchanging mindless pleasantries in such a state.

There was only one way to solve his current predicament.

He grasped his shaft, and then he closed his eyes once more.

A tempting heart-shaped mark on her throat…skin that smelled like the most fragrant blooms in the garden…

GRACE TOLD HERSELF there was only one solution to her current predicament. She had to replace all thoughts of Viscount Aylesford with something else. Fortunately for her, she knew precisely who could help her and how.

"You want to borrow *the book*," her sister, Christabella said.

"Hush," Grace warned, her gaze darting about the drawing room to make certain no one had overheard. They were in the midst of a heated game of charades, and seated near the periphery of the festivities where they could have private chatter, but one could never tell when other ears were listening.

"There is no need to flush and look so guilty," her sister teased quietly. "I did not say which book you want to borrow."

Her cheeks went hotter still. "You know very well which book."

Christabella was undeniably the wildest of the Winter sisters. Everything about her was bold, from her brilliant red hair to her manner. And so, it had surprised none of the Winter sisters one whit that it was Christabella who had been able to secure a set of books containing forbidden words and engravings.

Naughty, carnal depictions of men and women, to be specific. One of the words she had seen printed in the book returned to her then.

Coitus.

If their protective older brother Dev ever found out his sisters had procured such sinful literature, he would be furious. Which was why they had sworn one another to secrecy.

"*The* book?" Pru, the eldest of the Winter sisters, asked.

Of all the books Christabella had in her possession, there was one which was the most shockingly descriptive. One that had put them all to blush. One Grace had vowed she would never open again.

"Yes," Grace hissed, glaring at Pru. "*The* book."

"I thought you said you had no wish to read it," Christabella countered slyly. "I believe you called it rubbish."

"I called it nonsense," she argued, gritting her teeth. Of course, she ought to have known her sisters would not allow her to simply obtain the book with ease. "But the manner in which I referred to it matters not now. All that does matter is my necessity to borrow it."

"Why should you wish to borrow it?" Pru asked, her tone shrewd.

Pru always saw straight through to the marrow of them all. It was one of her gifts.

"I..." she stumbled about and then paused, searching for the proper phrasing. "Oh, very well. I require distraction."

"But I thought you said it was vile," Christabella said. "The sort of filth you would never deign to read again."

"Do hush," Grace grumbled.

"You called it offensive," Pru added. "The writings of a small mind. I believe you said it ought to be pitched into the ash heap."

It was true, Grace had been shocked by the words and images contained in the book. It was also true she had been curious about what those pages contained ever since she had ridiculed the book in question. For some reason, ever since Viscount Aylesford had begun paying her such marked attention over the course of this cursed house party, she had been thinking of the book more and more.

"I have changed my mind," she gritted. "I wish to borrow it. A day or two ought to be sufficient."

Yes, one day to remove all traces of Viscount Aylesford's handsome face from her mind. Two at the most. What she was experiencing was natural. An urge as simple as hunger. She would feed her curiosity using the book, and the impulse would be satisfied.

"What has changed your mind?" Christabella asked next.

"Nothing," she lied.

"It would not be Lord Aylesford, would it?" Pru whispered.

Drat the man.

"No," she fibbed a second time. "Of course, it is not."

"You did make a striking couple when you danced at the ball," Christabella mused. "And he is a rake."

Her sister sighed, for Christabella was of the mind that there was nothing more delightful than a rake. She had her heart set upon marrying one. Grace could not fathom why.

"Stop speaking about him," she ordered her sisters, all too aware of their audience and the carrying potential for their voices, even in a drawing room as massive as the one here at Abingdon House.

"She doth protest too much," quipped Christabella.

"Silence," she ordered her sister on another glare.

"I have the book," Pru said. "Pray, Grace, do not resort to pulling Christabella's hair."

"I have not pulled anyone's hair in years," she defended herself, miffed her sisters continued to bring up her means of girlhood defense.

When one came of age with four sisters, one had to make herself heard however she could.

"I will excuse myself and go get it," Pru whispered. "I will leave it beneath your pillow for safekeeping."

"Thank you," she said grimly. "You could have said as much from the first."

"It would not have been nearly as entertaining, however," Christabella observed, beaming.

"Or as illuminating," Pru added.

Sisters. Huffing a sigh, she turned her attention back to the proceedings.

But her mind continued to wander to those blue eyes to rival a summer sky and those sensual, smirking lips. To the sensation of a thumb brushing over her lower lip…

She could not get her hands on the dratted book soon enough.

BY A REMARKABLE stroke of fortune, Rand found himself alone with Grace Winter once more, and this time quite unintentionally. He had wandered into a writing room in search of his sister, only to find the chamber occupied instead by the auburn-tressed beauty who had been haunting his thoughts all day.

He should have observed propriety and left the room the instant he had seen it occupied by a lone, unwed female. But the female was Grace, and he had made a habit all his life of eschewing the proprieties altogether. Moreover, he needed to convince her to agree to be his feigned betrothed.

For reasons he chose not to examine, she was the only one who would do.

He closed the door at his back and strode into the room.

She had been seated, her head bent over a book, and at first, she did not realize she was no longer alone. Which was perfectly fine by Rand, as it meant he could leisurely drink in the sight of her as he crossed the thick carpets, his footsteps muffled. Her brow was furrowed, as if she were concentrating deeply upon something in whatever she was reading.

As he neared her, he realized there appeared to be an engraving on the pages she was contemplating. Before he could get a better look at it, she stiffened and slammed the book closed, alerted to his arrival at last.

"Lord Aylesford!" she exclaimed.

His title emerged almost as a squeak.

He was not certain if her discomfiture was a compliment

or an insult. He bowed deeply to her all the same, deciding he would do his best to woo her once more. They were nearly halfway through the duration of the house party already. His time to convince her of the wisdom of his plan grew more limited with each day that passed without a yes from her pretty pink lips.

And how he wanted a *yes* from her.

Lord God, how he wanted it.

A *yes* to everything.

But that would be dangerous. And foolhardy. And entirely damaging to his plan.

"Miss Winter," he greeted her in turn, deciding upon formality for the moment.

The moment and not a second more.

"What are you doing here?" she asked, rising to her feet with such haste, she upended her chair.

He decided her lack of composure was in his favor. She was flushed, her eyes wide, her lips compressed. She clutched the book she had been reading to her bodice.

"I am here in Oxfordshire to celebrate Christmastide," he said mildly, rather enjoying the sight of her flush expanding down her throat. He did not think he had ever seen her so flustered. "Mr. Winter and Lady Emilia Winter are hosting a house party. Perhaps you know them?"

She pursed her lips. "You have proven me right, my lord."

"Oh?" He sauntered nearer to her, drawn as ever.

Devil take it, but he could not expunge the thoughts of her which had brought him to release. Looking at her now, being in proximity to her, sent a fresh rush of lust pounding to his loins.

He had to stop.

"Your sallies are not humorous," she told him, still frowning, still clutching the book. "I was correct, of course. You rely far too much upon your handsome face."

He grinned. This was getting promising.

"You think me handsome, Grace?"

Her frown grew more severe. "*You* think yourself handsome. That much is apparent. And as we have already established, I never gave you leave to refer to me by my given name."

It nettled her when he called her Grace. He resolved to do it from this moment forward. No more *Miss Winter*.

"I was not making a statement, but rather posing a question," he prodded her. "I shall ask it again. Do you think me handsome, Grace?"

In truth, he did not merely think himself handsome. He *knew* he was. The females of his acquaintance had flocked to him. Always. He had no concerns in that quarter. The fairer sex found him impossible to resist. He had legions of bed partners to attest to that fact.

Which was just fine with Rand. It had always stood him in good stead. He had never gone without a woman. Had never had to.

All he required now was for *Grace* to find him impossible to resist.

Not him, he reminded himself sternly, but his *plan*. The plan was everything. The plan was all.

Tyre Abbey was his motivating force.

"I think there are some ladies who would undoubtedly find you attractive," she said then, interrupting his musings with her cool assessment. "However, I am not one of them."

The lying minx.

He moved nearer, thinking about the book, taking note of the protective manner in which she held it against her. Thinking of the engraving he had spied before she had snapped it closed. He had thought, for a fleeting second, that it had been a man and woman in *flagrante delicto*. But then, he had persuaded himself it was naught but his overeager imagination.

Now, he could only wonder.

"Forgive me, Grace," he said, stopping when they were almost touching. Near enough for her summer's blossom scent to envelop him. "But I cannot help but note the flush in your cheeks when you speak to me."

She frowned at him, moving away in a flick of her skirts, striding toward the opposite wall and her relative safety, he could only suppose.

"If I am flushed, it is because I am irritated," she tossed over her shoulder. "Nothing more."

"Or perhaps you are embarrassed by your attraction to me," he guessed, stalking after her.

She spun about so suddenly, he nearly collided with her. As it was, he was left reaching out to steady her, lest she lose her balance. Her soft arms burned his palms. Reminded him why he had spent that time in bed envisioning her sucking his—

"I am not attracted to you in the slightest," she told him, disrupting his thoughts as she wrenched herself from his grasp and put some more distance between them.

The stubborn wench was dismantling his opinion of himself, one brick at a time.

A cursed disconcerting situation, it was.

He decided to abandon that particular subject for the nonce. Instead, he turned his mind to the book. She had it pressed to her breast just now, and unless he was mistaken, he recognized that binding. He had seen that finely tooled leather before. The gilt title.

The Tale of…

The rest of the words were obscured by her fingers,

clenched tightly and protectively over the little book.

"Are you reading a volume of *The Tale of Love*?" he asked.

Her countenance went pale. "Of course not. What would make you think such a thing?"

He raised a brow. "The guilty expression upon your face, my dear Grace. To say nothing of the fact that you are familiar with the title."

The Tale of Love was a series of bawdy stories which had been published to great public outrage and scorn. They were supposedly the writings of a famed courtesan. Though no one knew precisely who had authored them, they were indeed lurid and shocking. In some instances, they were even downright depraved. The drawings which accompanied the stories were the stuff of legend. Rand himself had only been able to procure a copy *sans* engravings after the publisher had been jailed.

"I have no notion of what you are speaking of," she denied stubbornly.

But of course, she did. He knew it. She knew it.

Still, for some reason, he was determined to prove he was right to the both of them.

"Hand me the book," he said, holding his hand, outstretched, toward her.

Her sea-green eyes narrowed. "No."

Her lashes were long and luxurious. Her lips seemed fuller than ever, begging for his kiss. Being in the presence of Grace Winter was an exercise, all over again, in the knowledge he could not help but to lust after her.

"Give me the book and prove me wrong," he challenged anew.

"The book is not mine," she said, still holding it to her heart as if it were her most prized possession. "I cannot simply give it to you."

"Of course you can." He followed her to the opposite end of the writing room, not stopping until her gown billowed into his legs. "Extend your hand, offer me the volume you are holding, and there you have it."

"What I meant to say is that this volume is not mine to give," she said. "I am safekeeping it for a friend."

He raised a brow. "One of your sisters, you mean."

She stiffened. "Of course not."

A most unwanted thought occurred to him. "A gentleman friend?"

Her chin tipped up. "What if it is?"

Rand would tear the bastard limb from limb.

He gritted his teeth against a possessive surge he had no right to feel for a lady who had not yet agreed to become his feigned betrothed. "What is his name?"

"That is none of your concern, Lord Aylesford. Now please do go before someone finds us here alone together, and I am obliged to become your betrothed in truth."

She was maddening. Irksome. The most vexing bit of baggage with whom he had ever crossed paths. He wanted her lips beneath his.

Which was base foolishness, of course.

He needed to secure the estate, he reminded himself. He needed a betrothed to wave in Grandmother's face. The dowager duchess had been firm and stern in her demand. He *needed* Grace Winter. Some part of him was confusing his need of her assistance with his want of her. He had to make it stop. Surely there was another woman in attendance at this cursed country house party who could accommodate his desires.

When had he ever lusted after innocents? Never, he was quite sure.

Still, there was something within him, a hunger which

could not be quelled.

"I should think it may concern your brother to discover one of the gentlemen in attendance loaned you such an ill-suited piece of literature," he said.

The threat was beneath him. But he did not like to think of one of his fellow guests wooing her.

"There is nothing improper about this book," she told him, holding it to her as if it were a shield.

She was bluffing.

He reached for the book. Slowly, deliberately. Giving her time to retreat once more. She held her ground as he predicted she would, too proud to flee. He was already beginning to understand Grace Winter, he thought, and this would aid him in his quest to get what he wanted. Her cooperation.

And mayhap her lips.

Definitely her lips.

"If there is nothing improper about the book, you will not mind allowing me to see it," he reasoned smoothly. "Let go of your hold upon it, Grace darling."

"I am not your darling," she growled at him in her husky voice.

And damn him, but he could not help but to imagine hearing that dulcet tone say wicked things to him. Naughty, sinful words an innocent lady should never speak.

He tugged. "The book, Grace."

"You are insufferable," she said, sounding suddenly breathless.

Breathless, he could work with.

Excellent.

He was finally piercing her armor.

One more tug, and the book was his. A glance at the cover confirmed his suspicions.

"*The Tale of Love*," he read aloud, before flicking his

glance back to Grace. "Just as I thought."

Her color heightened. He wondered how far that delectable flush extended. But then he forced that thought from his mind. His prick was already hard enough. His breeches too tight. No thoughts of peeling her from her gown.

He needed her acquiescence.

And not, alas, in the bedchamber.

"Are you satisfied now?" she asked. "You were right. Now please do give me my book back."

"No," he said thoughtfully, a new plan forming. "I do not think I will. This is not fit reading material for an innocent lady. I am honor-bound to deliver the book to your brother and inform him one of his house guests dared to gift you with it."

Her lips compressed. "Do not do that, Lord Aylesford. Please."

"Call me Rand, Grace." He could not deny the appeal of hearing his given name on her sweet pink lips.

"No." She frowned.

Even her frown made him want to kiss her. Blast it all. He could not recall when he had last been so attracted to a woman.

"If you want this book, you truly ought to be more biddable," he told her smugly.

This was his revenge for the minx telling him to eat pie.

And he was enjoying it. Quite thoroughly.

"Biddable," she repeated, her lip curled. "Such a word has not, nor will it ever, be used to describe me, my lord."

"Rand," he persisted.

She moved suddenly, attempting to snatch the book from him. But he was quick, and he held it aloft, over her head. His formidable height had always stood him in good stead. Even rising to her toes, she could not reach it.

But fortunately, rising to her toes meant her body was pressed against his. Her breasts crushed into his chest. The scent of a summer garden hit him. He could not resist finding the small of her back with his free hand and holding her there. His cock was rigid, pressing into her belly.

A gentleman would have made an effort to hide his reaction to her.

Fortunately, he had never been a gentleman.

Her lips parted, her eyes going wide as they met his gaze. Understanding dawned in her eyes. "My lord…"

"Rand," he said again.

Curse it, there was nothing he wanted more than to take her mouth. Kiss her senseless.

"Give me back my book, Lord Aylesford," she said, her tone growing firm once more.

Willful chit.

He released her and stepped back lest his inner beast gave in to the need to taste her. "I will give it back to you on one condition: you agree to become my feigned betrothed."

"You scoundrel!" she accused.

And she was not wrong.

He grinned and bowed. "You have until tomorrow morning to consider my proposal, Grace. If you deny me, I am afraid I will have no choice but to surrender this book to Mr. Winter."

With that gauntlet dropped, he took his leave.

Chapter Three

"THAT MISERABLE CUR!" Pru said later that evening as the sisters gathered to prepare their *toilette* together before dinner.

Her tone of shocked indignation echoed through the chamber.

"He's an unabashed thief," Grace agreed.

Their lady's maids were not yet in attendance, and it was the perfect opportunity for sharing confidences amongst her sisters.

Namely, that Lord Aylesford had stolen *the* book.

"We must get it back from him," Christabella said. "If he gives it to Dev…"

All four Winter sisters shuddered at once. None of them wanted to even contemplate the notion of their beloved, overprotective brother discovering they were in possession of the notoriously wicked volumes of bawdy literature.

"Allowing him to go to Dev with it is an impossibility," Eugie said.

"Dev would have all our hides," Bea, the youngest of the Winter sisters, added.

Though Bea was already betrothed, and Eugie was perhaps on her way to becoming betrothed to the Earl of Hertford—in spite of Eugie's claims to the contrary—Dev would not allow any of them to escape punishment for such a daring violation of his edicts.

He aspired for them all to marry above their stations. And marrying above their stations meant they were required to act in strict accordance with societal mores. Innocent ladies were not permitted access to such forbidden words and pictures.

"Why did he take it?" Christabella asked then.

"Is that not clear?" Grace frowned, thinking of the ease with which the scoundrel had wrested the book from her grasp. "So that he could force me into doing what he wants."

"What is it that he wants?" Eugie chimed in, her tone suspicious. "He is not a fortune hunter is he, do you think? Revelstoke is rumored to be quite wealthy."

Aylesford's father, the Duke of Revelstoke, was indeed rumored to be flush in funds. As his father's heir, Viscount Aylesford should not be terribly in want of coin. Besides, he would hardly desire a betrothal he had every intention of breaking if that were the case.

"He does not wish me to marry him in truth," she told her sister, who was suspicious of all noblemen after an odious baron had spread lies about her to damage her reputation. "You know that, Eugie. He would hardly want to break the betrothal if he were a fortune hunter."

She and Eugie had discussed Aylesford's madcap plan at length, and while Grace had initially been considering the viscount's proposal—*er*, *feigned proposal*—she had quickly realized how dangerous engaging in such a farce could be for her.

Because he was more handsome than the devil, and he had more charm in his pinky finger than most gentlemen had in their entire bodies, and because she wanted very much to kiss him. In spite of all her common sense and excellent skills for rationalizing.

"More importantly," Pru interjected next, "why did you

take the book from your bedchamber? You knew the rules of *the* book, Grace."

Yes, she knew the rules.

And she had ignored them.

Her cheeks went hot. "I wanted to read it, and I could not seem to find a comfortable position in my bedchamber. The writing room has the loveliest desk and chair, and the way the afternoon sun pours in through the windows is so charming…"

"I have yet to hear sufficient reasoning," Pru pointed out.

As the eldest of the Winter sisters, she fancied herself their leader.

Grace could not argue with Pru in this matter, however. "I concede the point. I ought not to have taken such a risk by removing the book from my chamber. But I had no idea I would be interrupted by the viscount. And nor did I anticipate him wrestling it away from me and then using it as bribery. The man is more Machiavellian than I supposed."

"Or determined of what he wants," Christabella said on a sigh. "Which seems to be you, my dear. How thrilling! Aylesford is a notorious rake."

She fanned herself with her hand.

Grace scowled at her. "What is the matter with you? Rakes make abysmal husbands. All they do is chase after women until they make their conquest, and then they begin the process all over again."

"Rakes are silver-tongued devils," Pru agreed with more force than necessary. "Not to be trusted."

Grace eyed her elder sister speculatively. "Lord Ashley has been paying you a great deal of attention lately, Pru."

Pru's cheeks colored. "Lord who?"

"Lord Ashley Rawdon," Christabella answered before Grace could, issuing another sigh. "Yet another delightful rake in our midst. I do wonder at our brother's decision in allowing them *entrée* to this country house party."

"The reasoning is simple," Grace said, unable to keep a note of bitterness from her voice. "Our brother desires for us all to marry dukes."

"He is too late where I am concerned," Bea offered softly, smiling.

The youngest of the Winter siblings, Bea had fallen in love with a commoner like themselves, who also happened to be their brother's best friend and right-hand man. But Dev had made an exception because of the relationship he had with Mr. Merrick Hart and because of the undeniable bond Bea and Mr. Hart shared.

"You are sickeningly in love," Grace told her sister.

The twinge she felt was not jealousy, she reassured herself. Not at all. She had no intention of marrying. Since she was already assured of her portion of the Winter fortune, and since marrying a man would only put her at his mercy, Grace was merely riding out the storm of her brother's good intentions.

At least, she had been, until Viscount Aylesford had come along.

Until *Rand* had come along.

But no, she would not think of him in such intimate terms. If she must think of him at all, it would be as the varlet who had commandeered *the* book. The handsome devil who thought he could coerce her into doing his bidding. Never mind that she had been rather intrigued by the book she had previously disparaged. She needed it back in her possession if she and her sisters did not want to face impending ruin in the eyes of their brother.

"There is nothing sickening about love at all," Bea was saying. "It is actually the most wondrous feeling. The most frightening, as well. I was not initially certain I was what

Merrick wanted. All along, however, I knew he was what I wanted."

"How could you be so certain?" Eugie asked.

Bea gave them all a secretive smile. "I cannot adequately describe it. But when you know, it resonates in your heart. You simply know, the same way you know you must take your next breath. It is inescapable."

"It sounds like the plague," Grace muttered. "Or a raging house fire."

"Fatalistic," Pru suggested.

"Romantic," Christabella said.

"Frightening," Eugie added.

"Incredible is what it is," Bea countered, still smiling that secretive cat's smile of hers.

As if she knew all the answers to the mysteries in the universe. Which was utterly silly, considering she was the youngest of them all. What could Bea possibly know that the rest of them did not?

True love, said a taunting voice inside herself.

She told the voice to go to the devil. For there was no such thing as true love. She did not believe it. There was only the incessant need to convince one's self of a deeper purpose, she was sure.

She had no such need.

Her purpose was already true: she was going to collect her funds and live the rest of her life as…

Well, she had not decided that part yet. But she *would* decide it. She would find what made her happy, and she would do more of that. She would stay far, far away from dashing rakehells with black, wavy hair and sky-blue eyes. Rakehells who made her heart race with their mere presence. Who made her weak. Who stole her book.

The conniving bandit.

"Our lady's maids will be here at any moment," Pru said, interrupting Grace's wildly veering thoughts. "All this talk of love aside, something must be done."

"About *the* book," Christabella added. "It is so delightfully wicked. That volume, in particular, is a favorite of mine."

"It is a favorite of everyone's," Eugie agreed. "The pictures…"

"Oh, my yes," Bea chimed in on a sigh of her own. "Is that the volume that contains the story about the gardener and the lady?"

"It is," Grace confirmed, for she had been similarly mesmerized by the tale.

"I shall never think about a rose in the same fashion after reading that story," Christabella said. "What he did with the rose petals…"

"Was indecent," Grace interrupted sternly.

In truth, she had not found the subject matter of the book nearly as objectionable upon further examination. Indeed, she had caught herself envisioning similar scenes to those depicted. Scenes containing herself and none other than Viscount Aylesford.

"I was going to say it was intriguing," Christabella corrected, frowning at her. "Tell me you did not find it fascinating, Grace."

Of course she had.

Her ears went hot.

But she was not about to admit it aloud. Not to any of them, and certainly not to all her sisters at once.

"That is neither here nor there," Grace dismissed. "What matters is that the book is forbidden to us. It should not be in our possession, and if our brother knew it was, he would not stop until he discovered how we had managed to procure ourselves copies."

"Watson ought not to be punished," Christabella said, referring to her lady's maid. "She is delightfully enterprising, and she managed to gather the copies for us at great risk to herself."

"Watson cannot suffer for your carelessness, Grace," Pru said, pinning her with a distinctly unimpressed look. "If you had listened to me and kept it in your chamber, you would not be currently finding yourself in such a predicament."

"None of you shall suffer for my actions," she assured them, for she knew precisely what she had to do. She had to get *The Tale of Love* back from one thieving viscount. This very night. "I will make certain that nothing goes awry. I will have the book in my possession once more by tomorrow morning."

Eugie's brows snapped together. "Just what do you intend to do?"

Sneak into his chamber and steal the book back.

But she did not say that aloud, for she was no fool.

Instead, she gave all her sisters a reassuring smile. "I will convince him of the necessity of behaving as a gentleman. I will remind him he is our guest. Make him feel guilty in whatever sense I must."

"You are going to accept his plan to become his feigned betrothed," Christabella predicted with an air of firm conviction.

Why, oh why, did the mere suggestion make her pulse quicken and heat slide to her core? Why did the suggestion make her want him in a way she had never yearned for another man? Blast him. Was it his looks? His knowing air? Whatever it was, it could be ignored and dismissed. It had to be ignored, else she would become far too embroiled within it.

"I will do no such thing," she vowed. "It may have seemed appealing once, but I see the viscount for who and what he is.

I shall have no part of his plans, and he will return our book to us if forcing him to do so proves to be the last action I take."

The subtle knock of their lady's maids at the door heralded the conclusion of the conversation. But Grace's determination was renewed. She would get her hands on that book tonight. Whilst he was occupied with whatever it was that kept the gentlemen of the house party up all night, she would simply creep into his chamber, find the volume she was searching for, and leave.

Yes, she thought to herself, feeling quite pleased, this would be the proper way to regain control of the situation. All she had to do was hope nothing went wrong.

THERE WAS A female on her knees alongside his bed, her rump raised in the air. And, *Lord help him*, but he recognized those ivory satin skirts and that mouthwatering rump. He would recognize them anywhere.

Fortune's fickle wheel had finally given Rand a good turn.

That was the sole explanation for the presence of Grace Winter in his bedchamber this evening. She was still dressed in the luscious gown that had set off her figure to perfection at dinner. He supposed he could not argue with that, but he would not lie. Finding her naked, awaiting him in his bed, would have been an even greater treat.

This incredible view would have to suffice, however. The odds of ever seeing Miss Grace Winter naked, or in his bed, were indeed quite slim. He could admit these things to himself, if to no one else.

Thank Christ his valet, Carruthers, was nowhere to be found. The saucy chit would have caused the scandal of the age. What the devil was she doing in his chamber, anyway? And, more to the point, what was she doing beneath his bed?

Suddenly aware of the fact that he was lingering stupidly in the hall, where anyone could pass by and witness Miss Grace Winter's arse poking out from beneath his bed, he stepped over the threshold. After drawing the door closed at his back with as much haste as possible, he strode forward.

Drawn, it was true, by the mouthwatering sight of her derriere.

Her pale gown with its lace overskirt was a temptation pooled around her bent legs. Her arse was full and round beneath the fall of those skirts, raised as she moved about beneath his bed in search of something. *Lord help him*, but he wanted to cup her rump. To take it in both hands and squeeze. To lift her skirts to her waist, find the tempting flesh of her cunny with his fingers, part her, discover if she was as wet and hot as he suspected she would be.

Curse it.

His fantasy was getting the better of him. All he could think about now was raising her skirts and taking her from behind, there on the floor. Surely, she could not have planned such a display. He found it difficult indeed to believe that an innocent lady—even one from a family as notorious as the Winters—would have wedged herself beneath his bed in the hopes he would soon arrive and find himself unerringly tempted by the sweet curves of her bottom.

Which, of course, he was.

She had an arse he would love to spank. To caress.

New inspiration struck as he watched her wiggling about. Better yet, he could draw her to her feet, settle her palms upon his bed, kiss her throat right where that heart-shaped mark hid, and slide into her from behind while they stood there together.

But, no. Such thoughts were the work of the devil that sought to distract him from his course. And his course, as he reminded himself quite forcefully now whilst he stalked the rest of the way across his guest chamber toward her, was Tyre Abbey.

Not the beautiful, altogether wrong Miss Grace Winter. Temptation incarnate, though she may be. Amazingly, she had somehow failed to hear his entrance. He could only put it down to the size of the chamber and the softness of the carpet.

He could not stand here watching her rump, fantasizing about the different positions in which he could take her all night. Could he? His breeches were already far too snug.

"What the devil are you doing beneath my bed, Grace?" he demanded, his voice low.

She jerked, and then the unmistakable sound of her skull connecting with the wooden braces on the underside of the bed echoed in the chamber. Along with her muffled cry of pain.

"Christ," he muttered, dropping to his knees at her side. "Did you hurt yourself?"

She shimmied out from beneath the bed. Her cheeks were flushed, her auburn curls having escaped her coiffure to frame her face. She sat back on her knees as she rubbed her head, pinning him with a scowl.

"You need not have given me such a fright, my lord," she snapped.

The daring of this woman would never cease to confound him.

"You were beneath my bed," he pointed out. "What was I to have done? Begun disrobing whilst you were poking about under there?"

Now that he thought upon it, the idea was not a bad one. His fingers settled upon the knot in his cravat and plucked.

Her eyes went wide. "No disrobing, if you please, my lord. I merely meant to say you could have announced your presence with greater aplomb."

His cravat was undone, lying limply about his neck. Goading her was proving one of his favorite means of passing the time. "And why should I have to announce my presence at all in my own chamber, Grace?"

"Miss Winter," she corrected primly.

"*Grace*," he repeated, with delicious emphasis. "How else am I to refer to a female who has trespassed upon my chamber at such a late hour, hmm?"

She was still rubbing her head. "You know very well why I am here, Lord Aylesford. You need not play games."

"Oh, I play no games," he assured her, giving her a slow grin. "Does your head still smart, love? I can kiss it for you, to make it better, if you like."

"No." She was scowling at him again. "I would far prefer to suffer the headache, thank you."

"You wound me to my soul," he said.

But he was rather enjoying himself at her expense. Her reason for being in his chamber, and what she must have been looking for beneath his bed, hit him. *The Tale of Love*, that little bawdy book she was so intent upon regaining possession of.

"I did not suppose you had a soul," she quipped then. "Black-hearted scoundrel that you are."

He pressed a hand to his chest. "Whatever makes you think me a scoundrel? I am wounded all over again."

Her eyes were on his throat, lingering there. "You are attempting to bribe me into becoming your feigned betrothed."

He whipped off his cravat, discarding it somewhere over his shoulder. "I offered you an excellent bargain, Grace. Your cooperation in return for your bawdy book. An even exchange as it were."

"Why do you need a feigned betrothed so badly?" she asked.

"Good of you to ask." He shrugged off his coat, leaving him in only shirtsleeves and a waistcoat. "My grandmother, the dowager duchess, is requiring me to have a betrothed before she will allow me to take possession of Tyre Abbey."

"Tyre Abbey," she repeated.

He did not miss the way her gaze traveled over his shoulders.

Rand suppressed a grin and flicked open the buttons on his waistcoat. "An estate in Scotland. A wealthy one, but one that also has a great deal of meaning to me. I spent summers there as a lad."

He removed his waistcoat, sending it the way of his coat and cravat. There was a fire in his blood, a heat that seared him wherever Grace's eyes roamed.

And roam, they did. All over him.

Like a caress.

"Why are you disrobing, Lord Aylesford?" she asked.

"What else am I to do in my chamber?" he returned. "I am readying myself for slumber. You do not fancy I sleep in my clothes, do you?"

"But..." she sputtered.

"Grace Winter, bereft of speech?" he teased. "Let us mark this down in the annals of history."

"Very entertaining, my lord." Blushing furiously, she rose to her feet.

He followed suit, unfolding his legs to his full height. He towered over her. She was the perfect height for him. The air between them was heavy, tingling with a new awareness.

He found the short line of buttons on his lawn shirt,

plucking them from their moorings. "Have you made your decision?"

"My decision?" she queried, her gaze upon the swath of chest he had revealed.

Lord, her eyes on him were making desire turn from a flame into a raging fire.

"Will you agree to be my feigned betrothed?" he pressed, reminding himself that he needed her *yes* more than he needed her body.

More than he needed her lips beneath his.

Although, that was fast becoming a lie.

He grasped handfuls of his shirt and hauled it over his head. The shirt joined the rest of his garments he had already flung to the carpet. His love of sport had honed his muscles over the years, and he was well aware of the effect he had upon ladies, bereft of his clothes.

She did not answer his question. Her avid stare was consuming him.

He stepped toward her, prepared to take her in his arms. Everything in him cried out with want. He had thought he would seduce her into agreeing. That he would toy with her. Make her flush. Instead, he was losing control.

"Grace," he prompted, his voice thick with the desire burning inside him. "The choice is yours. Agree to be my feigned betrothed, or I will give the book to your brother. If you say yes, I will return the book to you at the conclusion of our betrothal, and no one will ever know your wicked little secret."

No one except for Rand, that was.

And he did not think he would ever be able to expunge from his mind the image of Grace Winter reading a bawdy book. Poring over an engraving of a man with his head between the thighs of a lusty lady. Or a lady with her lips wrapped around a man's cock. Or for that matter, the fantasy of Grace Winter's pouty pink lips wrapped around *his* aching cock.

Her stare jerked to his, and even this shared connection took his breath. Made him ache. Made him long for more.

"You promise to give me the book at the conclusion of the ruse?" she asked.

"Our betrothal," he corrected, noting the fashion in which she referred to his proposal.

"At the conclusion of this farce you have authored," she corrected, giving her eyes a dramatic roll heavenward.

As if she were frustrated with him.

When she was the one who was making him desperate for her, merely by her presence in his chamber. *Christ*, the scent of her would linger after she left. Summer blossoms and Grace.

Bloody delicious.

"I promise to give you the book at the end of our betrothal," he agreed, "or however you wish to refer to it. In return, you will agree to be my bride until I no longer have need of your assistance."

"Until Tyre Abbey is yours," she said, her gaze traveling once more. Dipping to his abdomen. Then lower. "How long do you think it will be? Days? Weeks?"

His cock was straining against the fall of his breeches.

"As long as it takes, Grace," he rasped with great effort.

The capacity for thought was fast fleeing him.

"Perhaps we should put a time limit upon my assistance," she suggested then.

If she didn't leave the chamber soon, his ability to resist taking her in his arms and kissing her senseless would be utterly nonexistent. As it was, he was calling upon every bit of his restraint.

"Perhaps you should say yes and return to your chamber where you belong before I completely disrobe," he countered, gritting his teeth. "Unless you wish to see my c—"

"No!" she squeaked. "I am going, my lord. I will agree to be your feigned betrothed in exchange for the return of my book."

He watched her flee from his chamber as if Cerberus were at her heels.

And as the door clicked closed on her retreating form, a river of regret flooded him. He rather wished she had stayed.

Chapter Four

"HE STILL HAS the book?" Pru asked the next day as they met in the library following breakfast.

Grace sighed. "Yes."

But she was not certain which was worse: the fact that she had given in and agreed to Lord Aylesford's scheme, or the fact that he had been pressing his cause by taking off his clothes.

She felt an ache deep within her even now, the next day, when he was nowhere in sight. Only a wall of books and her older sister about. He had been disrobing. And he had been beautiful.

One thing was certain: engravings on a page were no comparison to Viscount Aylesford in flesh and blood. He was all lean, powerful man. His abdomen had been accented by sinews and muscles, his chest broad and strong. The sight of him in nothing more than his breeches, which had clung lovingly to his strong thighs, had been enough to make her weak.

"And you have agreed to this plan of his, to pretend to be his betrothed, in exchange for his returning the book?" Pru persisted thoughtfully.

"I have," she admitted, still aggrieved with herself for her cowardly display the night before.

Still irked quite mightily by her reaction to the diabolical man.

She had conceded. Forgotten all about her quest to locate the book and circumvent him. Instead, she had wilted like a flower in the summer heat. She had run from him. Run from herself, as well. Because she had been terribly close to touching him. To throwing herself in his arms.

To kissing those rakish lips.

Pru cast her a sidelong glance as they walked along the wall of books. "Do you suppose Dev will be fooled?"

Grace swallowed. This was the part of the plan she disliked the most—deceiving her brother. Because she loved Dev with all her heart. He was a wonderful brother, and he had devoted his life to caring for them all. He only wanted what was best for them.

What he deemed was best for them, in some instances.

But his heart was pure, his motives true.

He simply wanted happiness for them all. Lying to him would not be easy.

"I suppose we shall have to see how successful Lord Aylesford is at persuading him," Grace said.

The viscount was smooth and charming. He was also the heir to a wealthy dukedom. Convincing Dev of the wisdom of a betrothal between himself and Grace would probably be easy. But their brother was also adamant that none of them would wed without agreeing to the match.

Which meant she would have to conduct an interview of her own with her brother. And hope he would not see through her deceptions.

"Have you ever wondered what it would be like to fall in love and marry?" Pru asked as they reached the end of the wall of books and paused.

There was no point in pretending either of them was searching for reading material. They had only sought out the room so they could have a moment of privacy to discuss the question of *the* book.

She gave her sister a searching glance. "Have *you* wondered?"

Pru averted her gaze. "Of course not."

"You have," Grace accused. "I can see it on your face."

"Oh, very well," Pru admitted. "I confess, I have found myself contemplating such a notion. Only with the right man, of course."

"Is there such a paragon in existence?" Grace could not help but ask.

For some reason, Viscount Aylesford rose in her mind. His handsome face. His dark hair, those blue eyes of his glinting in the candlelight as he had stripped off his shirt…

Foolish mind. The word paragon should never even occupy the same sentence as Lord Aylesford's name. He was a wicked rakehell. An arrogant oaf. He knew precisely how his masculine beauty affected all females in his presence.

"I think with the right man, it could not be as awful as I once supposed," Pru said then, her tone contemplative.

Grace raised a brow, considering her. "Has a gentleman in attendance changed your mind? Lord Ashley Rawdon, perhaps?"

The handsome Lord Ashley had been paying a marked attention to Pru. All the sisters had taken note of it.

Color rose to Pru's cheeks. "Of course not. Lord Ashley is trying to match me with his brother, the duke."

"Coventry?" This news surprised Grace even more. "Has he even spoken a word to anyone since he arrived at the house party?"

The new duke was painfully shy. Lord Ashley, however, was decidedly not.

"Scarcely a word to me," Pru said, "but I must admit, I

find myself wondering…"

"Lord Ashley is making you wonder," Grace predicted.

Pru frowned. "Perhaps Lord Aylesford is making *you* wonder."

"Do not be silly," she said, waving a dismissive hand. "I am only agreeing to this madcap plan so *The Tale of Love* is safely in our possession once more, without Dev ever being the wiser."

"If you insist, sister dearest," Pru said, sounding unconvinced.

"I do." She kept her voice firm. As firm as her intention to end the betrothal the moment Aylesford received Tyre Abbey. "There is nothing I like about Lord Aylesford at all."

Except for his handsome face.

Those sensual lips.

The way he made her feel.

And she could not forget his bare chest.

But she banished all those thoughts, for she could not afford to entertain them. The sooner her betrothal was announced, the sooner she could be done with this silly scheme and with Viscount Aylesford both.

If the notion sent a tiny pang of remorse through her, she chose to ignore it.

FACING MR. DEVEREAUX Winter and asking to marry the man's sister was rather a troublesome affair, Rand discovered. Perhaps it was because he had been seeking out Mr. Winter's sister without the benefit of a chaperone. Mayhap it was because he had spent the previous evening imagining all manner of wickedness concerning her after she had left his bedchamber.

Or, it was because he had no intention of actually marrying Miss Grace Winter.

Either way, he was having a difficult time refraining from shifting in his seat as he met Mr. Winter's gaze.

"You requested an audience with me, Lord Aylesford," Mr. Winter said, his countenance unreadable.

Well, perhaps not entirely unreadable. *Grim* might be one word Rand would choose to describe the fellow. *Murderous* was another. Though Winter was a massive beast of a man, Rand was strong. He had well-hewn muscles and practiced boxing regularly at the famed Grey's Boxing Salon in London. He could defend himself fairly enough in a match.

He cleared his throat. "Thank you for taking the time out of your hosting duties to meet with me, Mr. Winter."

"Excusing myself from a game of Bullet Pudding is no hardship," Mr. Winter said, unsmiling.

Christ. Rand had chosen his timing well, for he could not abide by most parlor games in general, but Bullet Pudding in particular. Anything that involved searching for a bullet in a pile of flour using only his face was not his idea of fun.

Still, to say as much would be unpardonably rude to his host and a slur upon his hostess, Lady Emilia Winter.

"Lady Emilia's entertainments have proven remarkably diverting," he offered politely. "I am sorry to be missing Bullet Pudding."

Mr. Winter tapped his fingers on the polished surface of the massive desk in the Abingdon House study. "Spare me the ceremony, my lord. Get to the heart of the matter, if you please, but I must warn you that if you claim to want to wed any of my sisters, I will find myself hard-pressed to believe you."

That revelation rather left Rand speechless for a moment.

He caught himself and carried onward. "I cannot fathom

why, Mr. Winter. Your sisters are all ineffably lovely ladies. Any gentleman would be pleased to take one of them as his wife. Myself included."

Mr. Winter's lip curled. "Your reputation precedes you, however, Aylesford. You are a notorious rakehell."

Devil take it.

He had not envisioned such outward hostility. Of course, he had never before asked for a lady's hand in matrimony, either. He had never supposed he would, until Grandmother had decided to use her power over him as if he were a mongrel she must bring to heel.

"I am not a rakehell, Mr. Winter," he defended himself. "Nor, surely, am I notorious."

Mr. Winter eyed him dispassionately. "Do not argue with me, my lord. It will not aid your cause."

He decided to try a different approach. "Mr. Winter, during the course of this house party, I have been charmed by Miss Grace Winter. I am determined to make her my wife, with your permission."

"No," said Mr. Winter flatly.

"No?" He sat up straighter, outrage stiffening every part of his body. "Mr. Winter, I am a viscount in my own right and the heir to the Duke of Revelstoke. What fault do you find with me?"

"There is much to find fault with from where I sit," Mr. Winter told him, his lips compressed, jaw tight. "However, the reason I do not give you my immediate permission is that I must hear from Grace herself that this is what she wishes. Contrary to what some may believe of me, I am not simply seeking to obtain titles for my sisters. I am wishing to find them husbands who will care for them and who will lift them up rather than bring them low."

"I am confident Miss Winter returns my feelings of deep

esteem," he said, wisely refraining from mentioning the reason for his confidence.

The bawdy book currently in his possession.

What Devereaux Winter did not know could not hurt him.

Winter gave a short nod. "If Grace confirms what you have told me, I see no reason to deny the betrothal. But know this, Aylesford: if you ever hurt her, if you ever make her cry, I will come after you."

Relief filled him. Not at Winter's threat, of course. But at his capitulation.

Victory would soon be his.

And not long after that, Tyre Abbey.

All whilst managing to escape the lifelong pain of the parson's mousetrap.

He grinned at Devereaux Winter. "I can assure you, I will never make her cry."

Winter remained as forbidding as an executioner. "I will see that you do not, my lord. Trust me on that score."

"YOU ARE CERTAIN this is what you want, my dear?" asked Grace's sister-in-law, Lady Emilia Winter.

They were in the yellow salon, surrounded by pastoral landscapes and the winter's sunshine filtering into the room through the westward-facing windows. The viscount had apparently wasted no time in seeking out Dev to ask for her hand, once he had been assured of her cooperation.

She loathed being dishonest.

Detested misleading Dev and Emilia.

But Lord Aylesford—that handsome, unrepentant scoundrel—had *The Tale of Love*. And she had no choice but to carry on with his plan.

To be fair, his plan was not entirely despicable. She had not been pleased with her brother's attempts at securing a match for her. Some part of her rejoiced at the notion of becoming betrothed. It would provide her with a respite from the attentions of suitors at the house party. Most of them were fortune hunters. All of them seemed to want to marry a Winter for the wrong reason.

"Grace, dearest," prodded Lady Emilia. "You did not answer my question. Are you certain marrying Lord Aylesford is what you want?"

Of course not. But she was not marrying him anyway.

"Yes," she said, pinning a smile to her lips that she hoped was bright and convincing. And deliriously happy.

She was doing her best to imitate the expression Lady Emilia wore whenever she spoke of Dev. Even if it made her want to gag, just a bit.

"Are you in love with Lord Aylesford?" her sister-in-law asked next.

"Of course," she lied again. "He is so very charming and handsome. How could I fail to fall in love with him?"

"You seem the least likely of all your sisters to fall prey to a rake's charm," Lady Emilia observed. "If I am doubtful, that is the only reason."

"You think Lord Aylesford is nothing more than a charming rake?" she asked before she could think better of the question.

In truth it mattered not.

She was not even wedding the viscount in truth.

This was all false. Feigned. Pretend.

One big deception, dreamt up by the silver-tongued devil in question.

"I think Lord Aylesford is exceedingly handsome," Lady

Emilia said with great deliberation, "and that he may easily turn a lady's head. He will also make an excellent match for you, as he stands to become the next Duke of Revelstoke. However, I cannot help but to be concerned that his lordship will break your heart. His reputation is questionable."

His chest, however, was not. It was delectable. Indeed, Grace could think of no other word to sufficiently describe it. And she had thought of precious little else ever since. Every other thought consisted of Lord Aylesford sans shirt, waistcoat, and cravat. Wearing nothing but those well-fitted breeches…

Grace wisely refrained from saying so, however. It was altogether inappropriate, anyway. She could never admit she had been alone in the viscount's chamber with him. That he had begun disrobing before her.

Had she lingered, the breeches would have been next.

She was sure her face was aflame.

"His lordship is the man I wish to marry," she said.

Strange how the words did not feel as foreign as she had supposed they would.

"You are utterly certain, Grace?" Lady Emilia asked, her tone one of sisterly concern.

Grace was heartily glad Dev had found such a kindhearted wife. Though she was an aristocrat and the daughter of a duke, she had warmed to Grace and her sisters almost instantly. Their bond was strong and true. And Lady Emilia's love for Dev was undeniable. It was the rare sort of passion that seemed to only grow as time went on.

The sort that only existed in novels.

"I am certain," she lied to her sister-in-law, reminding herself of all the reasons why this feigned betrothal with Aylesford was a good idea.

Listing the reasons in her mind…

The viscount would return the book to her, with Dev none the wiser.

She would no longer be required to suffer potential suitors during the course of her feigned betrothal.

She would be able to carry on with whatever she wished and follow her heart after the betrothal reached its inevitable end.

No more guilt and responsibility.

Being betrothed to Aylesford would not be entirely awful. He was ridiculously handsome, after all. And perhaps she would have the opportunity to kiss him. To touch him. If she wished, that was.

She did not wish, she told herself.

Oh yes, you do, said a voice from deep within. It decidedly was not Pragmatic Grace.

She chased the voice away.

Lady Emilia's gaze searched hers, almost as if she doubted the truth of Grace's words. "You are *completely* certain, Grace?"

Grace blinked. Was Aylesford truly that much of a reprobate? Her knowledge of his past was admittedly limited. All she knew was that he was a rake. And that he held an incredibly high opinion of himself. Not that such an opinion was unwarranted, but it went against the grain. She could not help but want to topple it.

"I am completely certain that I wish to wed Lord Aylesford," she fibbed, smiling.

Her lips were stretched so wide, her cheeks ached.

Lady Emilia frowned at her. "Very well then, my dear. I will inform your brother of your decision, and your betrothal will be announced this very night."

"This very night?" she asked, before she could think better of the words.

In truth, if she were indeed pleased by the prospect of becoming Viscountess Aylesford as she had pretended, she would like nothing better than for the announcement to occur with all haste. Instead, the mere mentioning of it filled her with misgiving.

But it was a feigned betrothal, she reminded herself.

Nothing about it was real. She would cut the ties with Aylesford as soon as she could. And she would be all the better for it.

"The betrothal will be announced tonight," Lady Emilia confirmed then, her expression sympathetic, her gaze searching. "You are still sure, my dear?"

"Sure," she echoed.

Even though something deep inside her suggested she was anything but.

Chapter Five

THE HOUR WAS late. The night was cold.

But Rand found himself outside, in the snow-covered gardens, just the same. Smoking a cigar. Pacing through the holly bushes. Wondering at his decisions. Confounded and elated and desperately wanting Miss Grace Winter all at once.

He puffed on his cigar, blowing smoke into the moon-bathed sky. The little clouds drifted heavenward, leaving him behind, mired as ever in his thoughts.

The entertainment of the evening had been a ball.

During which, Mr. Deveraux Winter had announced the impending nuptials of Rand and Miss Grace Winter.

He finally had secured his feigned betrothed, just as he had wanted.

And he had danced with Grace. They had taken their turn about the ballroom, but it had felt all wrong. As wrong as the announcement had felt. As wrong as every word of congratulations had felt. She had been somber and cool.

Something had nettled, deep within him.

Something that resonated even now, as he stood alone, in the unseasonably cold night air.

Something that felt a whole lot like guilt.

The unmistakable crunch of a footfall on snow behind him had him turning about. But the figure moving toward him was not masculine as he had supposed—a fellow gentleman seeking some night air after the ball's conclusion. So many dancers whirling beneath the chandeliers, coupled with negus and freely flowing wine, meant all the revelers had been flushed and overheated. Rand had been no different.

Unless he was mistaken, however, the shadowy form moving toward him was distinctly female. And familiar. All too familiar.

"Grace?" he asked.

"Lord Aylesford," she greeted in that husky voice of hers, which alone was enough to have his cock twitching to attention. "What is that wretched smell?"

Well, that was rather lowering. But his cock did not appear to mind.

"My cigar," he said, grinning at her cheek, the saucy wench. "What are you doing out here alone?"

"I am not alone," she returned, moving nearer, until the moon illuminated her sparkling eyes and her lovely heart-shaped face. "I am with you, my lord."

"All the more dangerous for you and your reputation," he countered, taking another long drag from his cigar before puffing it into the sky.

"Surely you are not any more dangerous to me now than you were before," she countered, tilting her head back.

Her lips were delineated in the moonlight, luscious and full. Those lips had been taunting him all night long. Calling to him. Asking him to claim them. He did not think he had ever wanted to kiss a woman more.

Instead, he continued on with the cigar. Because he knew that if he kissed her once, he would not stop. And if he did not stop, he would be facing far greater problems than convincing his grandmother to surrender Tyre Abbey.

"It is unwise to be alone with a man, Grace," he told her

softly. "Especially when that man is me."

"But you are my betrothed," she protested, a tinge of bitterness in her tone.

"And if we are caught together, we will be forced to wed." He inhaled once more, wondering why the notion of marrying Grace did not fill him with as much trepidation as he might have supposed it would.

She shivered. "That would indeed be a dreadful fate. Point well taken, my lord. I have taken all the air I need, especially since it is putrefied with the acrid scent of your cigar. If you will excuse me..."

She dipped into a hasty little curtsy.

But before she could flee, he caught her elbow in a tender grasp, staying her.

"A dreadful fate, Grace?" he repeated, her words nettling him in spite of himself.

To say nothing of her condemnation of his cigar. The wine had not been enough this evening, and sometimes when he needed to clear his head, a cigar was just the thing to bring him clarity and calm.

"Yes," she agreed. "Dreadful. I cannot imagine being shackled to a rake such as yourself, Lord Aylesford."

"Shackled?" He stubbed out the glowing end of his cigar in the snow lining a nearby statue of Apollo. "A strong choice of words, love."

"Helplessly tied," she suggested. "Chained. Inextricably bound. Which would you prefer, my lord?"

"I would prefer for you to call me Rand," he said, leaving the cigar abandoned at the god's feet.

She did not retreat, but held her ground. A cold wind blew, and she shivered again. He placed his hands on her upper arms. Her wrap was not nearly thick enough to weather the cold.

"Bloody hell, Grace, what are you doing out here without a proper pelisse?" He shrugged out of his coat and placed it over her shoulders.

Another gust of wind bit through his shirtsleeves, but he did not give a damn.

"I did not think to be out here long," she said. "I was overheated after the ball, and I could not sleep. I thought to get some restoring air, but then I saw you out here, standing alone beneath the moon."

"And you came to me," he concluded, warmth hitting him somewhere in the vicinity of his heart.

"I saw something glowing," she said. "I thought you were the devil himself. Do take your coat back, Aylesford. You'll catch your death if you do not take care."

The minx.

"You knew it was I when you came to me," he pressed, needing, for reasons he had no wish to examine, to hear her make the admission. "And as a gentleman, I insist you keep the coat on. I cannot have my betrothed contracting a lung infection."

"I knew it was you," she admitted softly. "You must be cold, my lord. Please, do take back the coat at once."

He had on gloves, a hat. But the wind was indeed beginning to cut through the wine-soaked warmth permeating his body. Then again, perhaps not all the warmth was down to the negus he had swilled at the ball. Likely, it had far more to do with the alluring woman before him.

He was still stroking her arms, he realized. She wore no hat, and with the next burst of wind came a torrent of snow flurries. Some of them caught in her auburn curls, glistening like tiny stars fallen from the heavens.

"Let us go inside," he said. "The weather is worsening."

"In a moment," she said, her voice hushed, her face upturned. "It is beautiful, is it not?"

"It is," he agreed, swallowing. But he was speaking about far more than the snow.

Flakes swirled around them in the darkness, gently falling. Kissing his cheeks, his nose. One landed on his lip. Gentle stings.

"Almost magical," she whispered.

Any good intentions he might have had fled in that moment.

If he did not take her mouth with his, then and there, he would surely die.

"Grace." Her name was torn from him. A warning.

"My lord?" Her gloved hands had come to rest on his shoulders.

She was in his arms. Where she belonged.

He struck that last thought away.

"I am going to kiss you," he told her.

Miss Grace Winter did not say a thing. Instead, she wound her arms around his neck and tugged his head down to hers.

LORD AYLESFORD'S MOUTH was on hers, his smooth, warm lips claiming. Sensation burst open. There was the cold of the night, the snowflakes falling all around them. The heat of his kiss. Fire licking through her.

He tasted of spiced negus and tobacco. Of sin and the forbidden. Dangerous and delicious.

All her good sense warned her to stop. Reminded her that kissing a rake like Aylesford could only lead to ruination. That she should not have sought him out in the moonlight. That they could be caught, and being caught was a risk far too ruinous to take.

But she had never felt more alive than she did now, beneath the wintry moon, the cold such a stark contrast to the fire heating her blood. *She* had kissed *him.* Or perhaps he had kissed her first? The moment had been so raw and visceral, awash with sensation, she could not be sure. Even now, her wits were jumbled, the only coherent thought rattling about in her mind *him.*

Whichever of them had sealed their fates, it had been a mistake, she was sure. But he had been so determined to warn her off, and since he had stolen the book from her, all attempts at putting a halt to the disturbing way he made her feel had failed.

This was his fault, really, she told herself.

And in fairness, he had made the announcement first. What was she to have done? Grace Winter did not flee from adversity.

The kiss changed. It deepened. He spun her around, and suddenly, her back was against the base of the statue of Apollo, which had been presiding over them. They were nestled between twin ivy hedges sculpted like obelisks. Trapped by his big body and with the surrounding foliage of the evergreens, she no longer felt the bite of the wind.

Instead, all she felt was him. His chest—the wall of muscle she had not been able to cease thinking about ever since she had first seen it the evening before—was flush against her breasts. He surrounded her. And then, he consumed her.

His lips were knowing, slanting over hers. She opened beneath his sensual onslaught, and his tongue swept inside her mouth. She had never before been kissed, but she understood now why Christabella would swoon over the affections of a rake.

If every rake kissed the way Lord Aylesford did, she would

happily spend each and every day being kissed silly.

At least, that was the way she felt now, in the madness of the moonlight, snow swirling around them, buffeted by holly bushes and midnight velvet sky overhead. That was the way she felt, in this man's arms, his mouth upon hers. Not even the cold winter's air could sway her.

Not even her rational mind. Not even her natural distrust of all noblemen in general and all rakes in particular. Not even the sure knowledge that Lord Aylesford was wrong for her, that he was only using her in order to obtain a property. That their betrothal, like this kiss, was fleeting, nothing more than a chimera.

But then, everything altered once more.

Because his hand slid beneath the layers of his coat and the cloak she had hastily donned before slipping into the darkened gardens. And he found her breast. Cupped it gently, rubbed his thumb over her nipple.

New heat sparked to life, traveling from the distended peak of her breast straight to the forbidden place between her thighs. A steady ache—the same that had plagued her whenever she thought of the viscount—turned into a pulsing throb.

A sound tore from her throat, and before she knew it, she was behaving in the same fashion as one of the ladies in *The Tale of Love*. She was arching her back, seeking more of that divine contact. Needing more of the pleasure he promised.

Kisses like this were why respectable ladies were ruined. Why sin was so promising a lure. Why resisting rakehells proved impossible for so many, despite all the warnings and tales of woe.

Grace kissed him back, learning from him how to move her lips in unison with his. She even dared to flick her tongue into his mouth once. And then again, because he groaned, and pressed her closer. And because the telling rise of his manhood was pressing against her belly.

She thought for a wild beat that she would not mind being wed to Aylesford. That surely there would be worse fates than tethering herself to a man who kissed so sweetly, who turned her body into flame by the mere touch of his lips to hers.

But then, another gust of wind hit them from nowhere, and suddenly, the last voice she wanted to hear severed the moment.

Her brother's.

"Grace!" her brother called. "Are you out here?"

She wanted to ignore him. To pretend she had not heard.

But Aylesford had heard it as well, and she knew it when he stiffened and tore his mouth from hers. His breathing was harsh, falling over her lips. Such warmth in comparison to the cold. Their eyes met and held.

"Grace!" called Dev. "It is too deuced cold for you to be out in the gardens on a night like this."

"Bloody hell," the viscount cursed. "Who is calling you, Grace? Another suitor? I will not have you making a fool of me during our betrothal. If that is your aim, you may as well cry off in the morning."

Indignation rose within her, swift and strong, chasing the dangerous desire which had been humming through her. She stepped away from Aylesford, wishing she had not fallen prey to his kisses quite so easily. Forcing herself to recall his impossibly large sense of his own attraction.

"It is my brother, you bounder," she whispered. "Stay here and say nothing. I will go to him."

"Grace," he protested, reaching for her, regret coloring his voice.

"Hush," she hissed, sidestepping him once more. "If you

alert him to your presence, my brother's wrath will be the least of your worries."

How dare he suppose she would become betrothed to him—albeit a feigned betrothal—and then meet multiple suitors in the gardens? Why, did he not know it was winter? And snowing? And the midst of the night? No sane person would go about dallying in the gardens with multiple men on such an evening.

Indeed, no sane person would go about dallying in the gardens with one man on such an evening. Particularly a handsome rakehell with the devil's own reputation. Which meant she was mad.

And she could not argue with herself over the reasoning.

"Grace," he said again, striding toward her once more.

But she did not want to hear anything he had to say. And neither did she wish to linger in his intoxicating presence for another second more. To do so would be foolhardy.

She turned on her heel and fled, rushing through the snow-covered path with such haste that she slipped and nearly fell. She caught herself just before she went careening into a holly bush, and almost slammed into her brother's tall, imposing form as she rounded a bend.

"Grace," Dev said in his familiar, comforting baritone. He gripped her by the elbows, steadying her lest she topple over as another strong gust of winter's wind hit them with full force.

How cold the night was, and yet, she had scarcely noticed the frigid temperature mere moments earlier, when she had been in Aylesford's embrace. Belatedly, she realized her toes were nearly frozen within her slippers. And Aylesford, the scoundrel, had assumed she had been meeting another suitor.

Good heavens, she had not even wanted the one, feigned suitor. *Er,* betrothed. *Er, feigned* betrothed. This was growing more confusing by the moment.

"Dev," she said, out of breath from her flight.

And guilty. Guilty as sin.

She could only hope the darkness of the night—in spite of the full silver moon hung overhead—would hide her flushed cheeks from her brother's all-too-knowing gaze. The last thing she wanted was for her brother to force her into nuptials with Viscount Aylesford.

"What are you doing out here?" her brother demanded. "You will catch your death if you do not take care. Or at the least, you will find yourself hopelessly compromised. Since your betrothal was only just announced this evening, I cannot help but to point out how foolhardy and reckless such a lack of care on your part would be."

She knew her brother well enough to understand he was suspicious.

"I was overheated in the wake of the ball," she said, which was only one-half a prevarication. "I merely came out here to cool off. To get some much-needed air."

"Much-needed," he repeated, his tone grim.

Oh dear. This did not bode well.

He offered her his arm, and she took it, allowing him to shepherd her back inside the sprawling manor home of Abingdon Hall. The door he chose entered into the study. When they were safely back inside, a wall of warmth hit her, emanating, no doubt, from the merrily crackling fire in the grate.

She could not deny the pleasure of the heat on her icy cheeks, or the bliss of it curling around her frozen fingers and toes. Her gloves had been donned for the elegance of a ball, not for the fierce cold of the winter.

The door clicked closed behind them, and she could not help but to think of the viscount, moored out in the gardens, all alone. Cold in the frigid winter's wind. He would find his way back inside. Of course, he would. But some part of her she had not previously realized existed had emerged, fretting over him.

After all, he had given her his coat.

Dear God, Aylesford's coat.

She was wearing it now…

Dev glowered down at her in the low light of the study. "Would you care to explain your foolishness tonight, sister dear?"

She cleared her throat, hugging the coat about her. A hint of his scent—amber and bay rum with that elusive tinge of musk, clouded by the tang of tobacco smoke—washed over her. She could not help but to inhale slowly.

The man smelled as delicious as he looked, curse him.

But her brother was towering over her, fierce and forbidding, demanding answers. Where was the calm, collected influence of her sister-in-law when one needed it?

"Where is Lady Emilia?" she asked, all too aware that her voice emerged as a squeak.

"In her chamber, preparing for a night of rest," he snapped, raising a dark brow of recrimination. "Just as you ought to be, Grace. Tell me, why are you not in your chamber?"

Briefly, she wondered—nay, hoped—that perhaps he had failed to notice the coat hung about her shoulders. "I already told you, Dev. I was far too warm after the ball, and I ventured into the gardens to seek some fresh, restorative country air."

"Indeed?" His nostrils flared as he posed the one-word question.

"Yes," she managed.

But her brother was far too wise for her ruse. He tugged at the coat still wrapped about her shoulders. "This belongs to

Viscount Aylesford, unless I am mistaken. And if I am mistaken, we have an even greater problem facing us now than I feared, Grace. So, tell me, if you please, which gentleman in attendance at this house party did you meet alone in the gardens? And which gentleman offered you his coat?"

She stared at her brother, stricken by the turn of events. When she had gone into the gardens, she had not bothered to think about consequences. And when she had realized she was not alone, that the male figure in the distance, smoking a cigar and so handsome in the silver light of the moon, had been Aylesford, she had not stopped. She had merely gone to him. She had been drawn to him, it was true, in the same way she had been drawn to him from their first dance together at the Welcome Ball.

"You are lying to me, Grace," her brother said sternly.

And he was, of course, not wrong.

Her older brother was protective and wise. She should have known better than to suppose she could fool him, or to think he would fail to notice the coat draped over her shoulders as boldly as any battle flag.

She sighed. "I am being truthful. I went outside for some fresh air. I was overheated. The wintry air quickly cooled me. But then, I noticed I was not alone. Lord Aylesford was already in the gardens, yes. However, we most certainly did not arrange for an assignation. I can assure you that nothing untoward occurred. He merely gave me his coat so I would not be cold. That is all."

Dev's countenance turned stern. "Grace, I want the best for you."

She bowed her head. "Yes, Dev."

"Look at me."

She jerked her head up, forcing herself to meet her brother's gaze. "I am looking."

"I am doing my damnedest to make our family—the reviled Winters, whose names are darkened by trade—proper. I want doors to open to us all. I want the *beau monde* to welcome us. I want happiness for us all, free of scandal, free of the shadows of the past." Her brother paused, seeming to gain his stride then. "But this cannot be accomplished, and it cannot be done, if any one of us embroils the rest of us in scandal. Not myself, not Prudence, not you, not any of our sisters. It cannot be done. Do you understand, Grace?"

She nodded, guilt weighing her down, sending any lingering traces of hunger for Aylesford scattering. She had been foolish and reckless tonight. She would not tread such dangerous ground again. That much, she vowed to herself, then and there.

"I understand, Dev," she said. "Forgive me, please. It was not my intention to cause a scandal or bring shame upon the rest of you. I would never have sought out the viscount in such a fashion. But since he was already there…"

"I know the power of attraction, Grace," her brother said wryly. "I am pleased that your feelings for Aylesford run true, because I had my doubts until tonight. But take greater care of your reputation for the duration of the house party. If not for your sake, then for the sake of your sisters. Please?"

He'd had his doubts until tonight?

For some reason, the urge to correct her brother's assumptions hit her. She was not so helplessly attracted to the viscount that she could not observe the tenets of propriety. No, indeed. Why, she could prove just how in control she was. Quite easily. One arrogant, handsome viscount was not enough to undo her.

Still, she knew now was not the time to argue.

Instead, she dipped into a curtsy. "Of course, Dev. I hold you and our sisters highest in my esteem always. You have my promise that I will not act so rashly in future."

"Promise?" he pressed, searching her gaze, his jaws clamped tight.

"I promise," she echoed, meeting his stare, unflinching.

At long last, it seemed he had the answer he sought.

"Excellent. Now, if you do not mind, it would not do for you to be seen running about the halls wearing your betrothed's coat." Her brother paused, his expression shifting, growing even more solemn. "Unless you want a scandal and a hasty wedding."

"No," she rushed to reassure him, moving to the side, before shrugging the coat from her shoulders and stepping away. "That is not what I wish. My only wish is for happiness for all of you."

"On that matter, we are in accord, dear sister," Dev said, still studying her, as if he was not certain if he could trust her words, her actions. "All I have ever wanted for you all is to see you happy and settled."

Guilt, that constant pinprick within her, deepened.

She was deceiving her brother. Because she would not be settled when her bargain with Viscount Aylesford was done.

And neither, she was certain, would she be happy. Because those stolen kisses in the snow-drunk moonlight had changed something inside her.

Had changed *her*.

Forever.

Chapter Six

LATE THE NEXT evening, Rand was still cursing himself whilst he played *vingt-et-un* with a small group of friends in an effort to while away both his time and his shame. He had made an utter arse of himself yesterday in the gardens with Grace. Not for the first time. Nor, he was certain, would it be the last time. His instinctive reaction had been to believe her false, and he knew the reason why.

The reason was an old one.

Started long ago.

With the woman who had shown him first that love could not be trusted, that passion was never meant to last, and that he must always guard his heart. Lady Georgina Duckworth, now the Duchess of Linden, had taught him a lesson he had never forgotten in all the years since.

Regardless of the reason for his assumptions, Grace had been giving him the cut all day long. He knew why.

"Aylesford," prompted Lord Ashley Rawdon, who was acting as dealer. "It is your turn."

He examined his cards, then flicked a casual glance over the cards of the players around him. The Earl of Hertford had already folded. The Duke of Warwick—Rand's oldest and best friend—looked smug. The Duke of Coventry, a painfully shy fellow, appeared morose, the three cards he had face up on the table either the sign of a winning hand or the sign of a man who did not know how to play *vingt-et-un.*

Rand could not be certain which it was.

His own hand scored only twelve, which meant he needed to risk another card.

"Another," he told Lord Ashley.

With a flourish, Lord Ashley turned up a card before Rand.

An eight.

Perfection.

If only his heart were in the game, one he ordinarily enjoyed playing. Another round, and Coventry folded. Warwick showed a nineteen. The initial stirrings of victory were sweet, precisely the distraction Rand needed. But when Lord Ashley at last flipped over his card to reveal he had *vingt-et-un*, not even the perfection of twenty mattered. He had lost. He sighed.

How fitting. He could not seem to win for trying these days. He muddled everything. He was not meant to have kissed Grace Winter. Was not meant to take her lips beneath his, to slide his tongue against hers, to taste the sweet mulled cider on her tongue. Was not meant to know the tempting weight of her breast in his hand, or the knowledge that her nipples were responsive, hard little buds he longed to coax to attention.

Ah, bloody hell. His cock was twitching just thinking of her. Just remembering her sweet mouth moving against his. This would not do. He had to distract himself by some other means. Clearly the diversion of cards had not been sufficient.

"That is all for me for the evening, I am afraid," he said, before taking a heartening sip of brandy.

"Congratulations are in order for your betrothal," Lord Ashley said carefully, taking a sip from his own drink. "I must say, I never thought I would see the day you allowed yourself to get caught in the parson's mousetrap."

With good reason. Rand was convinced never to consign himself to such a miserable fate.

However, he was determined to keep up appearances. If his plan were to be a success, it was imperative that the truth never reached his dragon of a grandmother. Only Hertford and Warwick, aside from Grace herself, knew the truth of their feigned betrothal. Hertford because it had been his idea, and Warwick because he was Rand's closest friend. Not to mention that Warwick was intending to marry Rand's sister Lydia, which practically made him family.

"Thank you for the congratulations," he said mildly. "Miss Winter persuaded me of the error of my previous ways."

Lord Ashley raised a brow. "You were betrothed once before, were you not, Aylesford? Miss Winter must be persuasive indeed if she convinced you to have another go at that infernal institution."

"Here now, there is nothing infernal about it," Warwick defended.

"I will second that," Hertford added, before casting a sly look in Rand's direction. "Do you not agree, Aylesford, now that you have newly joined the ranks of gentlemen who have fallen in love at this house party?"

Blast Hertford, whose plan to gain himself a wealthy betrothed had led to him falling madly in love with Miss Eugie Winter. She seemed the least likely match for the man known as the Prince of Proper. But Hertford had taken to wearing his heart upon his sleeve.

Warwick was no better, mooning over Lydia like a puppy in love with his new master. All rather disquieting, given that Lyd was Rand's sister and Warwick his friend. Even more disquieting since Rand himself had long since been cured of the belief in love.

He tossed the rest of his brandy down his gullet, searching for a suitable response. "True love finds us when we least expect it."

There, that was noncommittal enough. Utter tripe. He reached for the decanter, needing to refill his glass. The day had been a long one, and the night was proving longer still.

"There seems to be something in the food," Lord Ashley agreed then, his lip curling. "Do you suppose Deveraux Winter put some sort of poison in the dishes he is serving, to rot men's minds and make them more susceptible to matchmaking?"

"Grim thought," said the Duke of Coventry, who was far more soft-spoken than his outlandish rakehell of a brother. "Unlikely, however."

"No such poison exists," Hertford said, grinning, "else all the marriage-minded mamas would have armed themselves with it long ago."

Love *was* the poison, as far as Rand was concerned.

"Three of the five Winters are betrothed," Lord Ashley pointed out. "There are only two remaining, and my brother has his heart set upon making a match with the eldest of them, which means there will soon only be one."

"The eldest?" Warwick asked, his brow furrowed. "I confess, there seems to be so many Winter sisters about, and as I have eyes for only my own betrothed, I have the devil of a time telling them apart."

"The long Meg," Lord Ashley elaborated.

Everyone knew who the tallest Winter sister was, as she stood a head above the rest. She possessed the height of her brother, but fortunately, a far more ladylike countenance.

"An excellent choice," Hertford told Coventry. "Miss Prudence Winter is quite kindhearted."

Coventry, ever sparse of words, merely flashed a tight

smile. "Quite."

"He has set his heart upon her, despite her outspoken nature," Lord Ashley said, his tone one of disapproval. "I told him he would do better to find a more biddable sort."

"Biddable and the Winter sisters are as disparate as fire and ice," Rand could not resist warning. "If Coventry is seeking a quiet bride, he would do better to search for one elsewhere."

"That is what I told him," Lord Ashley said, an edge to his voice, his jaw rigid as he exchanged a glance with his brother. "But he will not listen to reason. As I have promised to aid him in his cause, I can do nothing but sit idly by and watch him commit this folly."

"I need a wife," Coventry said. "You know this."

"Yes." Lord Ashley's lips twisted in a bitter smile. "Thanks to Father's profligacy."

"The sins of the fathers are oft cast upon the sons," Hertford said. "I understand your plight all too well."

Rand's father, the duke, was not a wastrel, *thank Christ.* In fact, unlike most peers in his acquaintance, he liked his father, which rather set him apart. He had no painful upbringing, no need for a wealthy bride to replenish the dust-ridden familial coffers.

All he needed was Tyre Abbey.

At least, that was what he told himself as he listened half-heartedly to the chatter around him and sipped at his brandy. But there was one face that rose in his mind, impossible to escape, regardless of how much he attempted to bury himself in drink and amusement.

That face was hers.

Grace's.

And the longing that rose within him with each new thought of her seemed to grow stronger and more vibrant. He had kissed her just last night. What they had shared in the gardens had left him wanting more.

But wanting more was foolhardy and reckless.

Lord Ashley raised his glass in a mock salute. "A toast to all of you. It would seem I am the only one of us who intends to escape this house party with his future intact."

Rand drained another measure of brandy, feeling even more grim than he had before. He had what he wanted, he reminded himself. Word had already been sent to his grandmother. Lord willing, Tyre Abbey would be his sooner rather than later.

And then, he and Grace could put an end to this farce.

Why the thought left him with nothing but a hollow ache in his chest, he would not ponder.

THE SISTERS ENDED the evening as they so often did—gathered together in one another's chamber. This time, they had all descended upon Pru's bedchamber for their meeting of the minds.

"Has he said when he will turn over *the* book to you?" Christabella asked Grace. "Now that you are betrothed and he has what he wants, I should think it only reasonable for him to make good on his word. What need does he have of the volume anyway? He is an experienced rake. Surely he is already in possession of the knowledge it contains."

Grace sighed. "He will not return it until he is assured his grandmother, the dowager, will bestow Tyre Abbey upon him. She would not do so until he could provide a betrothed."

"That vagabond," Christabella said.

"He is an utter pirate," Eugie agreed. "Surely being in a feigned betrothal with him cannot be worth it. Perhaps we should all just go to Dev and admit Lord Aylesford is in possession of *The Tale of Love* and that he is using it to force your hand."

"No," Pru said. "We cannot admit to having *the* book in our possession. Dev would be outraged."

"And he would demand I surrender the other books in the series," Christabella added. "If Grace had not been gadding about with it, Aylesford never would have discovered it in the first place."

"I fear I must agree with Pru and Christabella," Bea added. "If Grace lost *the* book, she has to pay the forfeit."

"Even if it means parading about in a feigned betrothal with a rake?" Eugie demanded, sounding indignant.

"Everyone else is right, Eugie," Grace intervened on a tired sigh. "I am responsible for Aylesford's discovery of *the* book, and I must make it right. Even if that means accepting his madcap bargain."

"You do not sound particularly displeased with the notion," Christabella observed, her tone sly.

"It is not a horrid idea," she found herself saying. "As I told Eugie when Aylesford first made his proposal to me, a feigned betrothal is not entirely without merit. I will not be forced to suffer through an endless round of suitors, and Aylesford will get the estate he wants. It will be mutually beneficial."

"Except for the part where he stole our book and used it as leverage against you," Eugie pointed out, her gaze narrowing. "I know he is friends with Hertford, but truly, the man is a scoundrel for sinking so low and taking advantage of the situation. I cannot fathom it."

"He is not as bad as he may seem," she defended.

Four sets of eyes swung to her, making her realize, belatedly, what she had just said.

She cleared her throat. "He is arrogant, it is true, and more than aware of how handsome he is. Pompous as well. But he can be quite thoughtful. Last night in the gardens, he offered me his coat and stood there in the frigid wind in nothing but his shirtsleeves."

Oh dear. This revelation, too, had been far too much information. More than she needed to volunteer to her sisters, certainly.

Her ears went hot.

"What were you doing alone with him in the gardens?" Eugie demanded.

"You kissed him," Christabella guessed.

The fire spread to her cheeks. "I did nothing of the sort." She licked her lips.

"You always lick your lips after you tell a lie," Pru pointed out.

"You do, Grace," Bea agreed.

"You definitely kissed him," Christabella crowed, clapping her hands excitedly. "Oh, do tell us what it was like, Grace. None of us has ever experienced a true kiss before."

"I have kissed aplenty," Bea and Eugie protested in unison.

Eugie's betrothal to the Earl of Hertford had just been announced as well. Three of the five Winter sisters were now engaged to be wed. Two in truth, one in deceit.

"The two of you have not been kissing rakes." Christabella waved a hand through the air, as if she were clearing away an undesirable scent. "Lord Hertford and Mr. Hart are both lovely, but according to everything I have read, rakes kiss far more proficiently than gentlemen. You must tell us what it was like to kiss the viscount, Grace."

"Lord Hertford is incredibly skilled at kissing," Eugie said, championing her new betrothed.

"As is Mr. Hart," Bea added.

"Nevertheless," Christabella said, warming to her cause, "they are neither of them rakes. I want to know what it is like to kiss a rake."

"Do stop reading those novels of yours, Sister," Pru said calmly, ever the voice of reason.

"I kissed him," Grace admitted, tired of the back and forth of her sisters arguing.

Silence fell.

All eyes were on her once more.

"And I liked it," she added. "Christabella, I cannot speak for all rakes, but I can assure you that Lord Aylesford kisses with remarkable aplomb. Indeed, I would have continued kissing him last night had it not been for Dev's timely interruption."

"That would have been quite foolish indeed," Eugie pointed out.

She raised a brow at her sister. "You are not telling me anything I have not already told myself, and quite sternly, too. There is simply *something* about the man. I cannot define it."

"Rakish wiles," Christabella suggested, sighing wistfully.

"A handsome face," Pru added. "When he holds you in his arms, you forget all the reasons why you should not trust him. Why he is all wrong for you."

"Yes," Grace agreed with her eldest sister, frowning. Once again, it seemed as if Pru spoke from personal experience. "Just what have you been doing with Lord Ashley?"

Pru colored furiously. "Nothing at all. Certainly not groping each other in the gardens at midnight."

"There was no groping," Grace denied. "Well, perhaps just a bit of touching…but that, too, was quite exceptional…"

She was thinking, of course, of Aylesford's hand on her breast. The knowing way he had cupped her there. But the liberties she had allowed him were dreadfully improper. And then there had come his stinging suggestion she had another suitor she had arranged a clandestine meeting with in the gardens. The reminder rather dampened any incipient stirrings of ardor she may have been experiencing.

"You must take care," Eugie warned her. "If you allow things to progress too far between yourself and the viscount, you will find yourself wed to him in truth."

Grace sighed, the shame and the guilt returning. "I know."

"There could be worse fates, surely," Christabella suggested. "Can there be anything more romantic than a reformed rake?"

"You need not fear for my reputation," she assured her sisters. "I am impervious to Lord Aylesford's charms. The only reason I succumbed in the first place was curiosity. Now that my curiosity has been satisfied, I shall never let him kiss me again."

"Or grope you," Eugie insisted, her tone stern.

"It was not groping so much as it was caressing."

"Grace," all four of her sisters chastised at once.

"No more," she reassured them. "You have my promise that I will carry on with this bargain, continue with this feigned betrothal for as long as it must last, and then I will regain possession of *The Tale of Love*. I will never again allow the viscount to do anything improper with me or to me. Are you happy now?"

Pru's eyes narrowed. "I supposed we shall have to be."

"Good," Grace said. "Now please let us seek out another topic of conversation."

Christabella started talking excitedly about a book she was reading, and the rest of the sisters reluctantly allowed the topic to be guided into much safer waters. Grace heaved an inward sigh of relief at the reprieve.

All she had to do was keep her promise.

And to do that, all she needed to do was stay as far away from Lord Aylesford as she could.

Chapter Seven

STAYING AWAY FROM Lord Aylesford would have proven far easier to accomplish if he were not awaiting Grace in her chamber when she returned there from Pru's. She stepped over the threshold, snapping the door closed at her back, and blinked, certain her eyes must be deceiving her.

Certain the inert form on her bed could not be real.

But his handsome profile was unmistakable, as were the wavy, raven locks falling rakishly over his brow. He was dressed in his shirtsleeves, waistcoat, and a loosened cravat, and his lower half was clad in nothing more than his breeches and his stockinged feet. His shoes had been neatly toed off at the foot of her bed.

He looked as if he belonged there. Someone had made himself quite at home, but she girded her heart against the sudden pang there. Entirely unwanted. Foolish and reckless and wrong.

As wrong as the viscount's presence in her chamber.

"Lord Aylesford," she said quietly, lest someone overhear her. "What are you doing in here?"

Still, he did not move.

Good heavens, was he ill? Had something befallen him? Despite her pique with him from the evening before, and in spite of all her reassurances to her sisters, she found herself going to his side.

Though, in fairness, the scoundrel *was* lying on her bed.

She stopped when she reached him, heartened by the sight of the rhythmic rising and falling of his chest and the sound of his breathing. He was not ill, it would seem, merely—

He let out a loud, undignified snore.

Merely asleep.

In her chamber.

She poked his shoulder with her forefinger. The heat emanating from his big body seared her through the fine lawn of his shirt. So, too, the strong and delicious rope of muscle leading down his upper arm.

"My lord," she tried again. "What are you doing in my chamber?"

He shifted. "Mmm."

The low sound of his voice was a pleasant rumble. Decadent to her senses. She could not deny the warmth it sent washing over her. The need unfurling from deep within her core. Nor could she seem to stop staring at his lips and recalling how they had felt, firm and masterful, moving over hers.

One thing was certain.

The viscount had to go.

She gave him another firm prod. "Lord Aylesford."

"Mmm," he murmured again, the sound so low and satisfied she could not quell the answering ache it produced within her. "Grace."

Her name.

He had said *her name.*

Was he dreaming of her?

Half-awake and half-asleep?

She was about to give him another poke when he shifted, his large hand going to the fall of his breeches. To the *burgeoning* fall of his breeches. Where his manhood was, to be precise. Where he was growing stiffer and harder by the moment.

Lord help her, but the sight of those long, elegant fingers stroking over his—she searched for the wicked word from *The Tale of Love* and seized upon it—*prick*…

She swallowed, frozen. Caught in the helpless throes of her own desire. Surely it was wrong to watch him thus. Just as wrong as it was for him to be in her bed. As wrong as it was for them to be alone.

"Grace, love. Kiss me," he said, his baritone nothing more than a velvet rumble. A promise of the wicked.

Her cheeks were on fire as her gaze shot to his face. But he was still sleeping. It would seem he was dreaming of her. She ought to be irked. But somehow, she could not summon up a modicum of irritation or outrage.

Another stroke of his hand goaded her into action at last.

She shoved his shoulder with more force than necessary. But her mind was warring with her body. Telling her she had to act and fast, or she would be running headlong down the path she had so recently promised her sisters she would not tread.

He jerked awake with a start, his eyes blinking open to reveal those sky-blue orbs that haunted her in her own sleep. His expression was confusion mixed with irritation—no doubt at being jostled awake so rudely.

"Grace? What the devil are you doing in my chamber again?" he demanded.

The utter rogue. His hand had not even strayed from the fall of his breeches.

"*You* are in *my* chamber, Lord Aylesford," she informed him, doing her best to infuse her voice with disapproval. "And that is a question I should be posing to you. How dare you sneak in here and make yourself at home upon my bed? If my lady's maid or anyone else had ventured in here and found you awaiting me, our feigned betrothal would turn into a real one all too soon."

"I am in your chamber, you say?" he asked, at last lifting his hand from where it rested over his manhood and scrubbing it along his jaw.

"Yes," she hissed. "And you must go. At once."

"Must I, though?" He flashed her a lazy grin that made a frisson lick down her spine.

Even dissolute, likely half in his cups, and trespassing in her chamber where he decidedly did not belong, the man was irresistible. And he knew it, which made her reaction to him all the more maddening.

"Yes, you must go now," she told him, shaking the spell he cast upon her from her mind. "Make haste, and do not allow anyone to see you. I refuse to allow myself to be forced into marrying a reprobate who has cozened me into accepting a feigned betrothal."

"A reprobate, am I?" He frowned at her, still looking flushed and sleepy and oh-so-alluring. "A cozening reprobate?"

Well, perhaps she was being a trifle harsh. But in fairness, she was desperate to distract him by how discomfited his presence in her chamber left her. And she was equally desperate to see him out of her chamber before the temptation he presented got the better of her.

Before she lost control and joined him on the bed. Before she kissed him again.

"A scoundrel," she amended. "But still, a scoundrel who must leave."

He stretched his arms over his head. "But this bed is so deuced comfortable, Grace. And I confess, waking up to your lovely face is dashed enjoyable. I could grow accustomed to this."

She flushed to the roots of her hair; she swore she did. There was something so intimate about the notion of Aylesford waking up to her face…it meant they were in bed. Together. And that other things—wicked things, the sort of things she had only read about in *The Tale of Love* or heard about from the talk with Lady Emilia—had happened.

There was that awful, burning curiosity roaring to life inside her once more.

The curiosity she had turned to *the* book to quell.

The very book Aylesford had thieved. She must not forget about that.

"You had best not grow accustomed to it," she snapped, shoving rudely at his shoulder once more. "You will most certainly not be making a habit of sneaking into my chamber and falling asleep in my bed. Do get up, Aylesford."

"Careful," he cautioned, rubbing his shoulder where she had pushed at his immovable form. "I am a delicate flower. I bruise easily, you know. And if I am bruised, you shall have to kiss me and make it better."

She glared at him even as the thought of kissing his bare shoulder sent heat sliding through her veins. "You do not resemble a flower in the slightest, my lord. Right now, you resemble nothing so much as a rake who has invaded my chamber quite against my will. And neither will I be kissing you ever again."

Her gaze lowered to his mouth of its own accord.

Fair enough. Perhaps that was a lie. She certainly *wanted* to kiss him again. Mayhap just once more. To remove him from her mind for good.

"Never?" he asked, giving her a sly grin. "Do not make vows you cannot keep, Grace love. Those kisses in the gardens last night are making a liar of you."

The kisses in the gardens.

How could she have forgotten she was vexed with him?

Her lips tightened. She gave him another swat. "Do not remind me of my folly. Move, Lord Aylesford. The hour is growing late and the chance of you being discovered here greater with each second you linger."

"The kisses in the gardens are the reason I sought you out," he said, his teasing air vanishing. He rose into a sitting position, swinging his long legs to the floor. "You have been avoiding me all day."

Yes, she had.

As much out of irritation for his assumption as fear she would be too tempted again.

"You accused me of having another suitor meet me in the gardens and intending to make a fool of you," she pointed out.

He winced. "Forgive me, Grace. I was a lout, and I know it. I have no excuse save that I was once played false."

He rose to his towering height then. The magnetism he exuded was so potent, she had to take a step back in retreat.

Just one, before she held her ground. "You were played false, my lord?"

"I was." His expression turned grim, the soft lines of slumber faded now. "A long time ago."

Someone had broken his heart, it would seem.

The realization left her bemused. And beset by another emotion entirely. She refused to believe it was jealousy, for she had no designs upon Aylesford herself. She had been forced into their feigned betrothal. The kisses they had shared had been a rare aberration. One which would not be repeated.

"Who was it?" she asked, in spite of herself.

"My betrothed," he admitted, before raking his fingers through his tousled waves.

He had been betrothed before. How sobering the knowledge was, and how strange. It also made her realize how little she knew of him beyond the days she had spent in his presence at the house party. Nearly a fortnight, it was true. Hardly enough to learn everything there was to know about him.

He looked to be all of thirty. Surely, he had lived a long and storied life before they had ever crossed paths. And even within that observation lay another sobering fact: she did not know how old he was. She scarcely knew anything about him.

Though she told herself it did not signify, that his past had no bearing upon her role as his feigned betrothed, she still could not help herself.

"You had a betrothed?" she asked, curiosity prodding her.

And something else as well. Something she refused to examine or acknowledge.

He inclined his head. "I did."

For all that he had apparently been in his cups when he had fallen asleep on her bed—or at least, that was what she supposed—he seemed alarmingly sober now. "Was she a feigned betrothed as well?"

His lips flattened, his jaw hardening. "No."

Interesting.

For some reason, the notion of Viscount Aylesford, the charming, beautiful rake who kissed her so passionately and made her feel everything she did not want to, falling beneath the spell of another woman set her on edge.

"Were you in love with her?" she dared to ask.

"I thought I was until I saw her in the arms of a close friend," he said, raising a brow, his tone bitter. "Needless to say, I realized the error of my ways at once. I no longer count the Duke and Duchess of Linden amongst my acquaintances."

Dear heavens. His betrothed had betrayed him with his

friend?

And, even worse, they were now wed?

Little wonder he had become a jaded rake.

"I am sorry, my lord," she said.

His lips twisted into a wry grin. "I am not. She saved me from a terrible fate. I would far prefer to discover my betrothed is faithless than to discover my wife is."

When he phrased it thus, she could not argue. Still, she sensed the lingering hurt underlying his words.

"Nevertheless, it must have distressed you, her betrayal." She paused, searching his gaze, seeing a new side of him that somehow lowered her defenses. He seemed more vulnerable. Less sensual, rakish god and more heartbroken, beautiful man.

"It made me realize love is a fiction," he said. "But that does not excuse my accusations in the gardens last night. I am sorry for suggesting you were meeting another. I know it was only your brother, who was likely following you about and noted your disappearance. I cannot blame him, for I would do the same for my sisters. Fortunately for me, Lyd is marrying Warwick, and Cecily is still in the schoolroom. But if I had a blackguard like myself following about either of them, even if he was their betrothed..."

"Dev is protective," she agreed softly. "And I forgive you for the suggestion. I understand now that it was your past and not your opinion of me which led to your remarks. I do hope, however, that you will learn to trust me. I may be nothing more than your feigned betrothed, Aylesford, but I will not play you false. Not now, nor ever. This, I promise you."

"I believe you, Grace," he said, more solemn than she had ever seen him.

His assurance filled her with a new warmth. A different sort of warmth. A dangerous sort of warmth. Her emotions rioted within her, out of control. The way he looked at her was making her weak. Or perhaps it was her attraction to him, which was steadily growing with each passing day.

"Thank you, Lord Aylesford." She swallowed again, battling down a sweeping rush of feeling she had no right to experience.

He was not her true betrothed.

Nothing passing between them now was real.

He had been tippling. Had he not?

She searched his countenance for signs of dissipation and could not find any. He seemed utterly unaffected. Awake and intense. And handsome, so very handsome.

She could not shake the feeling that this night was bound to end badly.

RAND HAD BEEN plagued by the suspicion, from the moment he had first risen that morning with a stiff cock and thoughts of Grace Winter on his mind, that the day was bound to end badly. But before him, surely, was proof of the opposite. Grace was staring back at him with such innocence. And yet also with such desire.

She was the one thing he should not want and yet the one thing he knew he needed to have. Which was precisely why he never should have come here to her chamber earlier. That he stood here in such tempting proximity to her now was down to his own recklessness.

He had consumed enough brandy earlier to dull his senses and his pride sufficiently. He had wandered into the wing of the sprawling Abingdon House where he knew he could find Grace's chamber. He had found it with ease—thank Christ for the name placards in the hall.

But she had not been within. After his disastrous attempt

at distracting himself with cards, he had decided to seek her out. To apologize and explain himself. And then, he had trespassed upon Grace's private territory. The room had smelled of her—summer blooms from the most glorious English garden—and he had found it oddly comforting.

So, too, her bed. The pillow where she laid her head at night had called to him. He had paced about for a few minutes before he had realized she would not be appearing any time soon. Weary, and oddly lulled into a sense of peace by his surroundings, he had toed off his shoes and slipped into her bed.

Foolish?

Yes.

Delicious?

Also, yes.

Did he regret it?

Hell, no.

In fact, if anything, he wanted to return to her bed now. With Grace, if at all possible. He had been enjoying the most decadent dream when she had jarred him into reluctant wakefulness. Grace had been kissing him as sweetly as she had in the gardens.

Only, they had been in the bright confines of a hothouse instead. Surrounded by lush blooms. The sun had been warm all around them. And her hand had gone to his cock, stroking. Inciting a fire within him. She had undone the fall of his breeches and taken him in her hand…

And then Real Grace had suddenly forced him awake, chasing away the glorious seductress of Dream Grace. He could not help but to mourn the loss of that dream, that phantom touch, even now. It had been so good.

Too good.

Undeniable.

He desired Grace Winter, with a strength and a ferocity he could not ever recall experiencing before. When he was away from her side, he convinced himself he could maintain his restraint. That he must not jeopardize their feigned betrothal. But now he was in her chamber, and he had just been shaken from the most glorious dream, and the feelings were haunting him still, lingering like the cockstand he could not seem to control.

An idea was brewing within him. A wicked one, it was true. But he was a rake, was he not? And though it was foolhardy indeed, he decided, suddenly and recklessly, to tell her. Then and there.

"I want you, Grace."

Her lips parted. "My lord, it is improper for you to say such things to me. Recall, if you will, that I am not your betrothed in truth. I must insist you go."

"Improper, of course, and you must insist, yes," he agreed, taking a step forward. Into her. Her skirts billowed around his legs. "But do you actually *want* me to go?"

Her luscious lips tightened. "You are arrogant, my lord."

He could not argue the point. "Perhaps."

"You have an exceedingly high opinion of your looks."

This, too, he could not refute. He was in possession of a looking glass, and he was all too aware of the fairer sex's reaction to him. He had learned, however, that not even a man's outward appearance could win a woman's heart. That in spite of his looks, in spite of the fact that he was to inherit a dukedom, a woman could and would still scorn and betray him. Georgina had proven it so.

But it was not Georgina facing him now. Instead, it was Grace Winter. And Grace Winter was a different woman altogether. She was a rare creature, unfettered and bold, not at all the standard lady.

"Do you not find me pleasing to look upon?" he goaded gently.

She flushed once more, putting some distance between them. "Undoubtedly, every lady does. I suppose I am no different on that score, but I shall not be the one to enhance your already insufferable vanity."

Of course, he knew she was attracted to him. Her response to him—the way she had kissed him—told him everything he needed to know on that account. But he could not resist pressing the matter, just the same.

"Ah," he told her as he slowly prowled nearer, hoping to discomfit her. "But you *are* different from every other lady, Grace. So very different."

And she was.

But Grace was made of sterner stuff than that. Had she made it too easy, this dance would have only been half as much fun.

"And you are a silver-tongued devil," she countered coolly. "Flattery falls off your tongue with ease."

"You have been thinking about my tongue, Grace love?" He could not resist teasing her. "How wicked of you."

Her color heightened, but she did not retreat. "I refer to your capacity for wooing the fairer sex, my lord. Not to…other matters."

He could not suppress his grin any longer. He was enjoying this banter and battle of wits with her, as always. And far, far too much.

"Have I, Grace?" He trailed his touch over her jaw, stopping at her chin. "Wooed you, that is?"

She swallowed, and his fingertips absorbed the vibration—the sign he affected her far more than she allowed herself to show.

"Yes," she whispered.

"I want to woo you more," he told her. "I want to woo you until you cannot think of why you are vexed with me. Until you cannot think of anything or anyone but me."

Oh, yes. He did. He should not want that. His rational mind knew it all too well. But the other part of him—the beast—wanted nothing but Grace Winter. Nothing but challenge and daring and recklessness. Nothing but sweet, seductive surrender. Her surrender. Her complete capitulation.

He should leave her here, and he knew it. He should walk out her door, sneak back to his own cold and lonely chamber, and forget ever trespassing here. Grip his cock. Spend into the bedclothes. Go to sleep.

But he did not want to do any of those things. He did not want to obey the proprieties. He did not want to leave Grace's side. He did not want to go back to his chamber alone.

Damn it all, he was having a cursed difficult time reminding himself that Grace was not his betrothed in truth. That this was all a pretense. A means to enable him to secure Tyre Abbey.

"This is dangerous," Grace said then. "We cannot continue on as we have been. Last night was an aberration."

But he heard the hesitance in her voice. He read it in her eyes. As a man who had devoted practically the latter half of his life to being a rakehell, he knew damned well that Grace Winter was his for the taking. That she did not want him to leave her chamber, despite what she had said.

He also knew he would not take her innocence. Could not. She would go to her husband—to the devil with the bastard—without a hint of guilt.

But that did not mean Rand was averse to seducing her. There were other ways, beyond the rendering of a lady's maidenhead, which could offer pleasure, both to Grace and to himself.

He cupped her face in both hands, holding her gently, forcing her gaze to meet him. "Was it, Grace? Are you certain you want me to go?"

He lowered his head, bringing their lips near, but stopping just short of kissing her.

Her breath puffed over his mouth. "I…"

She was at a loss. Her words never finished.

"Tell me to go," he urged her.

Because he was confident, it was true, that she would do no such thing.

"Go," she said.

What the devil?

"Truly?" he asked.

"Yes," she affirmed. "You must leave this chamber, for if you linger, we run the risk of my lady's maid discovering you here. And if my lady's maid finds you within my bedchamber, I need not tell you what will occur."

Indeed, she did not have to tell him. For he knew. They would be forced to wed. Though he was averse to the parson's mousetrap, he could not deny there was something about the notion of being forever connected to Grace that left him pleased.

So pleased.

Perhaps he was going mad?

If he was, madness had never felt so right. Nor so tempting.

"What if I do not want to go?" he asked, taking a grand risk. Because he wanted Grace Winter. Wanted her when he should not.

"Why would you not wish to go?" she asked, sounding almost desperate. "There is no reason for you to stay. We are not betrothed in truth. Nor would we ever suit…"

"We would never suit?" he asked.

He would beg to differ. They suited. They suited far too well.

Her eyes went wide once more. "Lord Aylesford, I must insist you relent."

"Grace Winter," he countered, "I must insist you refer to me by my given name. It is Rand. Try it upon your sweet pink lips. Go on, see if it fits."

The sweet pink lips in question pursed, the epitome of disapproval. "My lord."

"Rand," he countered.

"Lord Aylesford," she said pointedly. "You must leave."

"Kiss me first," he dared her. "Kiss me and then tell me I must go."

The color in her cheeks deepened as he had known it would.

"I have no desire to kiss you," she said coolly.

He would have argued the point, for he knew a bloody prevarication when he heard one, but he did not. Because in the next instant, there was a knock sounding at her door. Slow and soft. But insistent.

Damn it to hell.

Their gazes met and held. Perhaps someone had overheard their low dialogue. He half expected Devereaux Winter to be at the door.

"Answer," he whispered.

"Yes?" Grace called out, her tone remarkably calm.

"Miss Winter, do you need my aid?" queried a female voice from the hall. "You failed to ring for me, so I thought it best to come to you this evening."

Rand found himself suddenly, ridiculously jealous of the lady's maid who helped Grace to disrobe. Still, he was relieved it was not her irate, ham-fisted brother at the door.

"I do not need anything, Carlson," Grace called in a pleasant tone. "Thank you, but you are dismissed for the evening."

"As you wish, Miss Winter," said the servant from the other side of the door.

The sounds of her footsteps fading into the distance fell heavily between Rand and Grace. They had nearly been caught. One wrong word, one wrong move, and their secret would have been revealed.

The moment made him feel alive. A heady rush washed over him. His heart was pounding.

"There now," he said softly when no traces of movement could be heard in the hall beyond. "Where were we? Oh, yes, I recall. You were just about to kiss me."

Chapter Eight

GRACE STARED AT Viscount Aylesford, his words echoing through every part of her body, making her wicked. Making her weak.

You were just about to kiss me.

She had not been. Of course, she had not.

"As I remember it, I was about to shoo you from my chamber like a bothersome fly," she retorted.

But her words were soft instead of sharp. And her heart was thumping. And deep inside her, unfurled a weighty, delicious coil of desire. The truth was, she did not want Aylesford to leave. She wanted him to stay.

"A bothersome fly, am I?" He was grinning that wicked grin of his that never failed to make her ache for him.

How did he do it?

"Yes." *Be strong, Grace. Be firm. Stand your ground.*

He took her in his arms, and she went willingly, because her body was a traitor to her mind.

"Would a fly do this?" He kissed the tip of her nose.

It was not what she had expected after the passionate kisses of the night before. Her hands were on his shoulders. Try as she might, she could not think of a single reason why she ought to push him away. The surprising tenderness of the gesture had robbed her of all ability to protest.

"I can honestly say I have never experienced a fly landing

on the tip of my nose," she managed to say.

"What of this?" He kissed her cheek.

"No." He smelled so good. And beneath her tentative touch, he felt so good as well.

He stayed close, his lips grazing over her ear. "This?"

"No," she admitted.

The heat turned into a roaring fire, scorching her. Need burst open like a blossom.

His wicked lips found her throat, kissing a patch of skin she had never even known was so sensitive before. "Would a fly do this?"

"Aylesford," she protested, flustered. Flushed and longing.

How he undid her, and with such tremendous ease.

"Rand." He nuzzled her cheek. "You smell so damned good, Grace. Like summer. I want to eat you up."

"Rand," she echoed.

There, she had done it. She had given in and spoken his given name aloud. It felt wicked and wonderful on her tongue. It felt wrong and right all at once, much like being in his arms did.

"Brava, my dear." His voice was low, laden with seductive approval. "Was that so difficult?"

She shivered. Not because she was cold, but because his lips were lingering near her ear once more, and it was filling her with sensations the likes of which she had never before experienced.

The last of her resistance melted.

"Rand," she said again.

"Mmm," he said, and it was just as before, a delicious rumble from deep in his chest.

She thought of the way he had stroked himself in his sleep and said her name.

And then she grew bold. Bold and reckless.

"Kiss me," she told him.

She did not need to say it twice. He cupped her face in his hands and settled his lips over hers. The kiss began slow. A subtle exploration, as if he had all night. A gentle pressure, a slant of his lips.

She sighed into his mouth and opened, rising on her toes to press her mouth against his. She wanted more. She did not want restrained or tender. She wanted powerful, possessive, demanding.

She wanted him to eat her up, just as he had said he would.

To pitch herself headlong into his flame and get burned.

Tonight, he tasted of brandy. His tongue played with hers and she was bold, running hers right back along his. She suddenly felt as if she could not get enough of him. As if he were not near enough. As if she could not kiss him long enough or deep enough.

Hunger and frenzy mingled, uniting to become one.

He broke the kiss, gazing down at her with a glittering, blue stare. "Am I still bothersome, love?"

"No," she admitted, her lips tingling.

She was alive, the wickedness coursing through her undeniable. Hunger for this man. Need for him. Why did he have to be so dratted irresistible? So handsome and self-assured? How did he always know just what to say, precisely how to touch her?

Because he is a rake, cautioned Pragmatic Grace.

"Do you still want me to go?" he pressed.

It would seem he would not stop until he had her complete surrender.

And she was going to give it to him. Because how could she not? He had routed her so completely, made his way past all her defenses, torn down all the walls of reason she had built around herself until nothing else mattered.

Nothing but his kiss, his touch.

"I do not want you to go," she confessed.

"Thank Christ," he said, and then his lips were on hers again.

Some part of her knew she should put an end to this. Or at the very least ask him what his intentions were. She could not allow him to do the deed. To take her maidenhead. Kissing him was one thing…the rest was…

His fingers tunneled through her hair, tightening on her in a possessive hold and angling her head to accept the seductive onslaught of his kiss. He bit her lower lip. Desire rolled down her spine, pooled between her thighs in liquid heat.

The rest was…

Wonderful came to mind. Exquisite. Forbidden.

Everything she wanted.

He seemed to sense the torrent of emotion coursing through her because he tore his lips from hers once more. "You do not have to worry, Grace love. I will not make this betrothal inextricable."

"Inextricable," she repeated, her mind fuzzy and dazed, struggling to comprehend.

"I am not going to take your innocence," he elaborated. "All I am going to do is give you pleasure."

He was going to give her pleasure.

The beautiful man before her, Viscount Aylesford, unrepentant rake, arrogant lord, maddening, alluring, and everything she had never imagined she would want so desperately, had just announced his intent to give her pleasure.

"Yes," she whispered.

And then she kissed him.

There was no question this time of who kissed whom, of

who made the move first, of whose lips slammed upon the other's. It was Grace this time, all Grace, and she did not even care. Everything else fell away. The curiosity she had been doing her best to ignore was back and it was bolder than ever.

It refused to be ignored.

He growled low in his throat, and then his hands were on her. Everywhere, it seemed, but as the bodice of her gown loosened while they kissed, she realized he had been plucking the buttons from their moorings. Her gown fell to the floor with a swift rush of air. Her petticoats were next. Followed by her stays.

They were still kissing, moving toward the bed.

Rakes were incredibly skilled at divesting ladies of their attire, it would seem. But she was too busy kissing him to care. Her lips were swollen. His tongue was in her mouth. He consumed her, overtaking all her senses. His scent, his touch, his taste, the sound of his heavy breathing, their kisses, the sight of his eyes burning into hers.

He was kissing her with his eyes open, and she was doing the same. She did not dare close them for fear of missing out on one moment of this delicious embrace. Because surely this night could never be repeated. She would never again have Rand in her chamber like this, would never again be so thoroughly at his mercy.

The realization cut through her, filling her with regret.

He was kissing down her throat now, all the way to her collarbone, his knowing fingers plucking at her chemise. He pulled it over her shoulder, then bit her there. Nothing more than a gentle nip of his teeth, it sent longing arcing through her.

It occurred to her that he was disrobing her and yet he was still fully clothed. And then she thought of how beautiful he had looked that night in his chamber, his chest bare. She wanted to see him again. But this time, she wanted to touch him too.

She wanted the forbidden she had denied herself.

She reached between them for the closures of his waistcoat, then plucked them free, one by one. He shrugged it away, and then grasped her chemise in his fists. In one swift pull, he drew it over her head. Cool air kissed her bare skin. She was wearing nothing but her stockings and his stare heated as it traveled over her.

A sudden burst of panic hit her. He had seen other ladies naked before, surely. Many of them, if his reputation was to be believed. How would hers compare? Her limbs were too short and curvy, her breasts not as large as some ladies'. She attempted to cover herself.

He caught her hands in his and pulled them away. "Do not hide yourself, Grace. You are so bloody beautiful. More beautiful than I imagined."

He had imagined her nude?

The revelation gave her pause, enough that he took advantage of the situation and guided her back toward her bed. Her rump connected with the mattress.

"Get on the bed, love."

She was sure she should not. But she did as he asked, shimmying with as much elegance as could be mustered when one was clad in nothing more than her stockings with a gorgeous rake eating her up with his penetrating gaze.

He opened the handful of buttons on his shirt before hauling it over his head. And then he was on the bed with her. And on her.

"You are delectable," he said, awe in his voice.

His mouth was upon her before she could even form a coherent thought. But not on her lips. No, it seemed he was intent upon kissing every inch of her. His dark head lowered over her breasts first.

One thing was certain when his lips closed over the peak of her breast and sucked.

This night was going to end her.

FOR A BRIEF, wild moment as Rand sucked Grace's nipple, he was convinced he was dreaming. That was how good it felt to have her lush, warm curves beneath him. To have her naked and flushed, her eyes glazed with passion, her body answering his every caress. To swirl his tongue over the pretty pink peak of her.

But there was no denying the reality of the soft, taut bud tightening. Or the moan he wrung from her in the process. Nor the way her back arched, presenting both her breasts to him like offerings. Perfect handfuls, her breasts. Silken and round and oh-so-tempting. Creamy temptations topped with carnation-pink blossoms.

Another realization hit him as he devoted himself to the delicious act of torturing the other breast in the same fashion and earning another throaty growl from her in the process.

Her lips matched her nipples.

And they were every bit as delicious.

She was sensitive there as well. He rubbed his whiskers over them, testing her response. A breathy sound emerged from her. Learning everything about her was going to be a thrill unlike any he had ever known. With other lovers, he had never been so attuned to them. Nor had they been as exquisitely uninhibited as Grace was in her response.

It was because everything was new to her.

He was the first man to ever touch her thus. To take her nipples in his mouth. To own her body with his hands. To bring her to release. The last, he had not done yet, but he had every intention to this night before he left her bed.

Something about that knowledge heightened his desire. Lust coursed through him, so potent and aggressive his ballocks ached. His cock had been stiff from the moment she had woken him, and no respite was in sight. Because he could not breach her barrier. He could not take her as everything in him roared to do.

He could take this far enough. Just far enough to make her spend.

Preferably on his tongue.

But that would have to be all.

He sucked hard on her nipple, and she mewled, and then her fingers were in his hair, sliding through it. Her nails were on his scalp, a delicate abrasion he did not think he could ever get enough of. He blew on her nipple, then caught it between his teeth and tugged.

That made her gasp his name. "Rand."

God, yes.

He liked that. And so did she. He did it again. And then he did it to her other nipple as well while he rolled the abandoned bud under his thumb. She thrust her hips beneath him, as if seeking to be nearer. It drove the moist heat of her cunny into the fall of his breeches. Into his desperately straining cockstand. And she was so wet, her dew coated him, sinking through the fine fabric of his breeches. He rolled his hips against hers in response, grinding himself into her core as he sucked her nipple.

"Rand," she cried out.

The sound of his name in her dulcet voice made him harder still. He jerked into her, wondering how the hell he would ever make it through the night without sinking home inside her.

You cannot, he reminded himself.

She is an innocent.

An innocent he would dearly love to debauch, completely and thoroughly. In every way. He wanted to claim all of her. To make her his. To keep her beneath him, at his seductive mercy, to make her body on fire for him. To make her weak with desire.

But that was not to be.

She was his feigned betrothed. He was not going to marry her. He was only going to make her come, and then spend the rest of the night alone in his chamber, stroking himself into oblivion on thoughts of what might have been.

She moaned, her hips twitching. She was thrusting her cunny into his cock in a parody of lovemaking.

And if he did not take care, he was going to spend in his breeches like a callow youth without ever even tasting her there.

Or worse, they would get caught. How could he have known his Grace would be so ravenous, so responsive, so noisy?

His Grace?

The possessiveness he felt for her was absurd, and it distracted him long enough to allow her nipple to fall from his hungry lips. What the devil was he thinking? Had all the blood in his body rushed to his swiving-starved cock? He had not had a woman in… *God's blood*, he could not recall how long it had been.

He had parted ways with his last mistress and had fallen prey to ennui.

An ennui which was nowhere to be found tonight, in Grace Winter's bed. He had to taste her now, he knew, before he lost what little control he had over himself. He kissed his way down her body, caressing her everywhere as he went. The flare of her hips was a miracle. Her pale thighs were soft and supple beneath his hands and already parted as he worked himself there.

"Rand?" she asked. "What are you…"

He kissed her inner thigh. "Hush, Grace love."

He kissed the other thigh. Gently guided her legs farther apart. She was perfect there, pink too, a silken patch of auburn curls covering her mound. The bud of her sex was engorged, taunting him. Her scent reached him, flowers and woman. Sweetness and spice.

And he could not delay.

He lowered his head and flicked his tongue over her pearl. Gentle, rapid swipes at first, lapping at her, finding the most sensitive place.

"Oh," she keened, her thighs clamping on his head.

She did not need to try to keep him there. He was not going anywhere. Not until she was shaking and crying out and spending. He wanted to make her wild with need. To work her into such a frenzy, she came so hard she saw stars. That frantic thought foremost in his mind, he sucked hard on her pearl.

Sucked until she was bucking beneath him, shaking and crying out. She was spending already. Over the edge with the wildness of her release. He had not imagined she would be so quick to come, but since she had been, he would treat her to another.

With great pleasure.

Rand licked down her slit. She tasted so good. Better than the most decadent dessert. And the sounds she was making, the shudders rolling through her body, the thrusts of her hips, were building to a frantic crescendo inside him. He could not control himself. He was out of his mind for her.

He thrust his tongue inside her entrance, penetrating her

in shallow thrusts. She made a muffled sound of pure bliss. He glanced up at her, his tongue inside her, and their gazes met. She had pressed her hand over her mouth, presumably to stifle her cries. Her eyes were wide and glazed, the obsidian discs at their centers dilated wide with desire.

She was flushed, her hair wild about her face, her breasts thrust in the air, and her cunny his to devour. So, devour it he did. Until she was coming undone again. She shuddered and undulated beneath him, riding out another wave of pleasure.

He would have brought her to a third pinnacle, but he did not think his cock could withstand any more torture and denial. With great reluctance, he kissed her once more, and then kissed a path back up her lovely body before sprawling alongside her, his heart pounding. His ballocks drawn tight with the need for his own release.

One which would not be forthcoming.

He sighed. And this was why one did not dally with virgins.

But it had been worth it. So very worth it to be the first to make Grace spend.

Indeed, if he could do everything all over, he would not change a bloody thing. This small part of her, this memory, would always be his.

Even when she was not.

GRACE HAD BEEN right. This night had ended her. She had exploded into a thousand glittering shards of light. There was nothing left of her. Her heart was galloping. A warm, delicious glow suffused her body. The center of her was still throbbing with the incredible aftermath of what Rand had just done to her.

Yes, Rand.

He would be Rand to her forever now. She did not suppose she could ever think of him by his title now that his tongue had been inside her.

His tongue had been inside her.

Good God.

Slowly, the stupor of her pleasure began to ebb. Reality returned. With it, the realization she was naked save her stockings, and her feigned betrothed was clad in nothing but breeches, his bare chest pressed intimately to her side, his lips slick with her own dew.

She stared at him, at the shocking yet erotic picture they made, their bodies aligned almost as one, his so masculine and different from hers. And then she could not help but steal another look at his mouth. Could not help but to imagine it there, between her legs. Making her wild for him, bringing her to heights she had not known existed.

Nothing in *the* book had warned her about what Rand had just done to her.

Nothing could have prepared her.

But then she thought of other things she had read about in *The Tale of Love*. Specifically, actions a woman could take. Ways a woman could bring pleasure to a man. Her mind returned, inevitably, to the way he had been upon her entrance of the chamber. Asleep, moaning her name, stroking himself. Her gaze dipped lower and found the bulge at the fall of his breeches had not diminished at all.

If anything, it had grown more pronounced.

The sight sent a pulse to her core. To the place where he had licked and kissed and sucked her with such inspired abandon. That old curiosity was back. She could not help but to wonder what he must look like. The engravings in *The Tale of Love* were only so detailed.

She licked her lips before modesty returned to her. She was naked. Lying next to the viscount. Hastily, she plucked up a corner of the counterpane and drew it over her body, covering herself.

"You have no need to be shy, love," he said softly, pressing a kiss to her temple.

The gesture was so tender, very much like one a true betrothed would give to the woman he intended to wed. Her foolish heart gave a pang before she reminded herself none of this was real. Rand still had no desire to marry her. As soon as he had Tyre Abbey, their betrothal would be over.

Tonight had been a lapse of reason.

A momentary abandoning of her wits.

For a rake who had seduced and charmed his way through the ladies of his acquaintance, tonight had likely meant nothing at all. Nor could it mean anything to her. And neither could it be repeated, she admonished herself sternly.

"I am not accustomed to…this," she managed to say.

He caught her chin between his thumb and forefinger and tilted her face toward his. He was so unfairly handsome, it almost hurt to look upon him.

"You had better not be accustomed to any other man but your betrothed making himself so familiar with you," he said, his countenance grave.

"Feigned betrothed," she reminded them both.

His gaze searched hers. "I have never disliked the word *feigned* more than I do now."

Her breath caught in spite of herself. "And yet, that is the truth of our circumstances, is it not? Eventually, our betrothal must come to an end, and you and I will part ways."

His lips tightened. "That is the truth, yes."

"Will you ever marry?" she asked him on a rush, before she could withhold the question.

He said nothing for a time, the silence stretching between them so long she feared he would not answer. And yet, for all the quiet, he still remained at her side, their bodies touching from hip to shoulder. He still held her chin captive. Nor had he left her bed.

"I do not know the answer to that," he admitted at last, his voice nothing more than a rasp. "I suspect I will need to one day, to carry on the Revelstoke title. For now, it is a needless concern as my father, the duke, is hale and hearty."

For some reason, the notion of him marrying someone else, a nameless, faceless lady no doubt born to nobility and bred to be a duchess, irked Grace. Even though she knew it should not. Even though she had known, all along, that her betrothal to Rand was feigned. Even though she had not even wanted to be betrothed to him.

Little wonder ladies lost their hearts to rakes.

She had thought herself made of sterner stuff than this. But she was as weak-willed as anyone after a handsome man turned up in her chamber and made her drunk on pleasure.

Not just any handsome man, said that horrid voice inside her, the one which never relented. *Rand.*

"Were you dreaming of me, earlier?" she asked next, because it would seem there was no limit to her foolishness and recklessness this evening.

She had ruined herself. Allowed a man who was not her husband—who was not even her real betrothed—to undress her and take her to bed. To make love to her with his mouth.

And his tongue.

Her cheeks flushed.

"Yes," he told her. "If you must know, I was dreaming about you, Grace."

And then he did another thing most unlike a feigned betrothed. He tenderly brushed a tendril of hair away from her cheek and kept his hand there, caressing her as if she were precious to him. As if she were someone important.

Someone, even, he cared for.

"I know you were," she confessed before she could think better of the revelation.

He raised a brow. "How do you know that?"

"You were saying my name," she admitted. "When I first came into the chamber. You were saying my name and…"

"And?" he prompted, his tone going wicked once more.

All her good intentions faded. The heat inside her that had never died roared back into a pulsing, raging flame.

"And you were touching your…" She paused, allowing her words to trail off, not certain she could say the word aloud. It was too wrong.

"My?"

"Your prick," she said on a rush.

He stared at her, his expression unreadable. "Say it again."

She bit her lip, hesitating.

"Damn, Grace, you are not making it easy to remain honorable."

"Prick," she said.

He groaned softly. "I like it when you say naughty words. And when you bite your lip. And when you look at me that way."

"What way?" she asked, even though she knew she ought not.

"As if you want me to debauch you."

His words made a new wave of desire wash over her. The flesh he had brought to life seemed to be the center of her being. She was pulsing, aching. From nothing more than a sentence from him coupled with a ravenous look.

Because she *did* want him to debauch her.

Heaven help her, she wanted Viscount Aylesford—Rand—to debauch her in every way. But that would be more foolish than allowing him to remain in her chamber. More foolish than kissing him and letting him kiss her between her thighs.

"Maybe I do," she said.

After all, she did not ever need to marry anyone, in spite of her brother's aspirations for her. When she came into her majority, a sizeable portion of the Winter fortune would be hers. She could live as she wished. Not tending to orphans as Pru longed, and not as an *accoucheuse* bringing babies into the world as Bea wanted. She had not yet seized upon her path in life.

But when she found it, she would know, she was sure.

"Bloody hell, Grace," he growled, and then his lips were on hers. He kissed her long and deep and hard.

There was a new undercurrent to this meeting of mouths, an acknowledgment of what had passed between them. She tasted herself on his lips and tongue. It was at once both shocking and erotic. If he wanted to debauch her thoroughly all night long, she would not offer up one word of protest.

She ought to feel shame, and she knew it. But she could not summon up a modicum of it. All she knew was the vibrant, fiery need for him.

But he broke the kiss sooner than she would have liked, and without rolling atop her and stripping her of the counterpane as a wicked part of her had hoped he might. Instead, he pressed his forehead to hers, his breathing ragged.

"A new bargain is in order, it would seem," he said.

"Oh?" she asked.

"I will debauch you."

The dark promise in his voice was undeniable. But he had said *bargain*, had he not? Which meant he wanted something in return.

"And what do you require of me?" she dared.

He appeared to ponder her query before deciding upon his price. "A favor."

"Just one?"

"Yes." He kissed the tip of her nose.

"What is the favor you seek?" she could not help but to question. After all, it would be foolish indeed to agree to any sort of bargain with him before she knew the precise details.

Would it not?

What would be the harm? The voice inside her—the one she ought to ignore, the one that did not belong to Pragmatic Grace—asked.

"I shall tell you when I decide upon it." He disentangled himself from her and rose into a sitting position.

She rose as well, clutching the counterpane to her chest, hating for him to go. "That is hardly fair, my lord."

"Rand," he countered, "or no debauching."

"Rand," she agreed. Far faster than she ought to have. But her body had made her decision for her.

The curiosity he had brought to life needed to be answered.

By him. By Viscount Aylesford, jaded rake, handsome lord, wicked scoundrel, by *Rand*, who kissed her and made her melt. No other man would do.

He dropped a hasty kiss on her lips. "I must go now, for lingering here is a risk I dare not take. After all, we have tomorrow."

"Tomorrow," she repeated before she could even think better of the bargain she was agreeing to. Before sense or reason could weigh in and divert her from her course. "Yes."

He gave her a beautiful, wicked grin. And then he rose from her bed. She could do nothing but admire the muscled plane of his back as he sauntered off in search of his shirt and waistcoat.

The man was the very devil, she was sure of it.

But being wicked had never felt so right.

Nor had anything in her life outside of being in his arms.

Chapter Nine

RAND WAS A fool. That much was utterly certain.

He was also thinking with his cock rather than with his brain.

That was why, he told himself the next evening, he had once more slipped into Grace's bedchamber. Why he was once more tempting fate. That was why he had returned for more of her, even when he knew he was putting his future in grave danger by sneaking into her chamber.

Also, why he had managed to wheedle some information about her from the servants belowstairs. His valet, Carruthers, had done a damned fine job of ferreting out all manner of facts.

She was an early riser.

She deplored the color yellow.

She adored savoy biscuits.

She took her tea with sugar and milk.

She also enjoyed sketching.

And certainly, it was why he had managed to procure a gift for her from the village. Not as fine as what he could obtain in London, it was certain, but the handsomely bound leather volume with its blank, creamy pages would have to do.

He had not been this determined to please a woman since…

Christ, not even Georgina had inspired him to go to such

lengths. And any of the women he had known since had required precious little wooing. With his reputation, bored wives and demimondaines were eager to share his bed. Their relationships had been predicated upon the need to slake their mutual passions and nothing more.

None of those women had been Grace.

None could even compare.

He clenched his jaw so hard his teeth ached as he stalked the length of her chamber, clutching his gift for her as if he were some sort of lovelorn suitor. What the devil had he been thinking? And was it his imagination, or had she been paying far too much attention to Lord Ashley Rawdon during their earlier drawing room game of Forfeits?

He growled just to think of it.

The door clicked open at last, and there she was. Her eyes went wide, as they lit upon him, almost as if she had not expected to find him within. She did not hesitate, however. She swept over the threshold and closed the door at her back.

"Rand," she said softly, a tentative smile on her lips.

Lips he could not wait to feel beneath his again.

He forgot he was the experienced rake. In her presence, he felt as if everything was new. As if each look, every touch, each kiss, was unlike any other.

Belatedly, he realized he was still standing in the midst of her chamber, clutching the gift he had bought her, looking the fool.

He stepped forward, calling on all his charm. "I brought you something."

Christ. What manner of charm was that?

In her presence, he felt more like a callow youth attempting to woo his first lady love rather than the hardened rake he had become. He suppressed a wince as he held out the volume for her.

"A gift?" she asked, her smile changing. Deepening. "For me?"

"It is deuced improper, I know," he said, for it was considered *de trop* to gift an unwed female anything, and he knew it. Even one's betrothed. "But surely not any more improper than offering you a daily debauching."

She accepted the book from him. The rich green gown she wore this evening made her eyes an even darker hue, rather the color of moss deep in the forest. "Thank you, Rand."

"It is for sketching," he said needlessly, feeling suddenly awkward.

"It is lovely," she said, tracing the cover with her fingertips. "How did you know I like to sketch?"

He cleared his throat. "Do not all females like sketching?"

"I do not know," she said, glancing back up at him. "Perhaps they do."

Her gaze searched his, and once more, that strange sensation rose within him. The urge to please her. To make her happy. To see her smile. To be the man who put the color in her cheeks and the fire in her eyes.

"I may have inquired after your likes," he admitted, clasping his hands behind his back so he would not be tempted to touch her.

Debauching her would be slow and steady and delicious. He could not fall upon her like a ravening beast. No matter how much he longed to.

"And what did you learn about me?" she asked, a new smile flirting with those luscious pink lips of hers.

"You prefer to rise early," he said, "you do not like to wear yellow, you like savoy biscuits, and you take your tea with sugar and milk."

She raised a brow. "Were you interviewing my lady's

maid, my lord?"

He grinned. "My valet may have posed a question or two. Nothing at all untoward in a gentleman seeking to learn more about his betrothed, is there?"

"His *feigned* betrothed," she corrected him.

Blast. He did not need reminding. He already knew his time with her was limited. The more he thought about it, the more it nettled, in fact.

"No one else knows I am your feigned betrothed, however," he pointed out.

Her cheeks went red.

"Do they?" he prodded, suspicion blossoming inside him like a flower.

"No," she said quickly. Far too quickly. And then she licked her lips.

It was a nervous habit of hers he had noted before. Partially because staring at her mouth had become an obsession of his. Partially because he paid far too much attention to everything about her.

Enough to know when she was lying to him.

"Who knows, Grace?" he demanded.

She winced. "Only my sisters."

Her sisters? As in more than one? As in *all* of the bloody Winter females?

"Curse it, woman, you mean to tell me there are five other females in this household who are aware of the nature of our betrothal?" he asked.

"Only four," she dared to correct him. "There are five of us sisters in all, not six."

"It certainly seems as if there are more of you," he muttered. "A legion, at least, with all the troublemaking."

"That is unfair, and you know it," she said, sounding wounded. "None of us have made trouble."

He gave her a pointed look, sweeping from her auburn curls to her dainty, slipper-shod toes peeping from beneath the hem of her gown. "You are nothing but trouble, Miss Grace Winter. Look at you. You are the loveliest, most vexing, tempting creature I have ever beheld. You had but to ask for me to debauch you, and here I am in your chamber, your willing slave. At great risk to my reputation and future, I might add."

"I am trouble?" Both her brows went up. "You are a rake who forced me into being your feigned betrothed. You have me doing all sorts of things I promised myself I would never do. Also, at great risk to *my* reputation and *my* future."

When she was in high dudgeon, she was a sight to behold. Her cheeks were flushed, her eyes sparkling, one hand firmly planted on her hip in defiance. The stubborn, willful, wonderful woman.

She had cast a spell upon him.

Perhaps all the Winter females were witches.

That had to be the answer to this maddening effect she had upon him.

"Why did you tell all your sisters?" he asked. "You know very well that this charade of ours will only be effectual if everyone believes it is true."

"My sisters will not tell anyone," she said. "This, I promise you. Our secret is safe with them."

He did not particularly relish the notion of his future resting in the hands of five Winter ladies. For yes, he was including Grace in the count in this instance.

"It had better be safe," he warned, "or not only will I refuse to debauch you, but I will also be forced to turn your bawdy book over to your brother."

She smiled then, the minx. "Something tells me you would still debauch me just the same."

She was not wrong.

There would never come a day when the sun would rise and he would not also want Grace Winter. It was a devil of a realization to make.

Especially when he was standing before her in her bedchamber at close to midnight where he most definitely did not belong. And while she held the gift he had given her in her hands and looked so damn beautiful, his chest hurt just to gaze upon her. His heart was thudding fast. Another realization, one that was far more damning, loomed.

He dismissed it with action.

Silenced it with a kiss. His mouth on hers. How easy it was. How familiar and right, the way their lips fit together. As if this one set of pretty pink lips had been made by God just for Rand to claim and plunder and make his. More dangerous thoughts.

He chased these by sinking his hands into the silken web of her hair. Pins rained on the carpet. Her mouth opened. His tongue swept inside. He was here to debauch her, he reminded himself. Not to feel anything. Emotions were not for him. He had learned his lesson in bitterness and betrayal. Had learned the most difficult way possible that love was not real. That only lust was true.

Except…

Except, this did not feel like mere lust now, when he was kissing Grace. When she was kissing him back with a fervor and an innocent ardor that had his cock throbbing and standing at aching attention. One kiss. One melding of their lips. And he was rigid, his ballocks drawn tight.

He ought to have stroked himself to a spend this afternoon instead of submitting himself to silly games. Thinking of her that morning and taking himself in hand had clearly not been enough.

He forced himself to end the kiss.

She blinked up at him, her lips darkened and swollen, her expression dazed. She still held the sketchbook he had given her, and it was between them like a shield.

"You are right, Grace love. I will always want to debauch you," he told her, hating himself for the hitch in his own voice. How easy it was for the seducer to become the seduced when it came to her. He did not feel like an experienced rake. He felt like he was drowning in her, drowning in his need of her.

Or inebriated.

Delirious on desire.

On her.

She stroked his cheek. A gentle caress. There was tenderness in that lone gesture which set him aflame. "Thank you for the gift, Rand. I will treasure it always."

She did not need to fill in the remainder of her words, for he knew what she meant.

Even when we are apart.

Even after our feigned betrothal is at an end.

He swallowed against a rush of emotion he refused to acknowledge. He had pretended to be betrothed to her for a handful of days, and already, he never wanted this to end.

"You are most welcome," he told her thickly, before taking the book gently from her grasp and setting it atop a nearby table. "But now, I do believe the debauching must commence. We do not have all night, more's the pity."

RAND HAD MADE an effort to learn more about her.

And he had brought her a gift.

And her foolish, foolish heart was pleased. Her reckless,

naïve heart was feeling things. Bursting with them, in fact. Things she had no wish to examine.

Better to distract herself, she reasoned.

She had been thinking, all day long, about how she might bring him pleasure. She *wanted* to bring him pleasure. Grace glanced down at his breeches as he settled the gift he had given her upon a table. The fall of them was once more pronounced.

She mustered up all her daring and boldness. *The Tale of Love* had described a lady taking her head gardener in hand. They had been amongst the roses. She had undone the fall of his breeches and eagerly gripped his staff. She had then fallen to her knees, taking him in her mouth in loving fashion…

She closed the distance between them, her breasts colliding with his chest, and then she settled her hand over him there. The rigid outline of him pressed into her palm. A new sense of wonder rushed over her, along with an answering ache between her thighs. He was so large. And thick.

He hissed out a breath. "Fucking hell, Grace. What are you doing?"

The epithet should have shocked her, but it did not. *The* book contained such words. Filthy words. Delicious words. Tentatively, she stroked him through his breeches. He seemed to grow even larger.

"I am touching you," she said. "Do you like it?"

His hand closed over hers, and for a beat, she feared he would pry it away. But instead, his clasped it, pressing her more firmly into him. "I bloody well love it, but I am supposed to be debauching you, not the other way 'round."

"The gardener liked when the lady touched him thus," she told him. "In *The Tale of Love*, I mean. He also liked when she took him in her mouth."

He groaned as if he were in pain. "You ought not to have read such wicked things, love."

"Is it true?" she pressed, the curiosity which had been dogging her gathering momentum. "What you did to me last night…would you like if I did the same to you?"

Another gust of air left him. His gaze grew heavy-lidded. His eyes seemed to burn into hers. It was as if nothing and no one else existed beyond the confines of this chamber. As if they were alone in the world, as if everything had fallen away.

"Of course I would, but Grace, that is not why I am here," he said, his voice low.

"You are here to debauch me, are you not?" she asked.

"Yes."

Together, his hand atop hers, they stroked him again.

"Then debauch me, Lord Aylesford."

"Damn it, Grace," he growled. "This is not fair."

She smiled, sensing she was winning their skirmish. And then she rose on her toes, bringing her lips to his. On another groan, he devoured her mouth. She sucked on his tongue, desperate for him. For more.

She found the buttons on the fall of his breeches and began undoing them, one by one. As their tongues tangled, she discovered his hot flesh. He sprang forth, into her hand, long and thick and yet smooth as velvet. He guided her fingers around his shaft, showing her how to grasp him. How to stroke.

He moaned into her mouth, into the kiss. But this was not enough. She wanted to worship him in the same way he had worshiped her. She wanted to make him lose control. To reach the heights of bliss he had taken her to last night.

She broke the kiss. They were both breathless. Their gazes clashed and held. She lowered to her knees on the plush carpet.

"Grace," he protested. "You do not need to do this."

He was glorious, rising stiff and proud. She ignored him

and leaned forward, licking around the bobbing tip. The taste of him was too good, musky man, sharp soap. She glanced up at him, her hair falling heavy around her shoulders. He was so handsome, it almost hurt to look upon him.

"Do you like that?" she asked, uncertain of what she should do.

The book had said the lady took the man's staff in her mouth. But Rand's staff was large. She did not see how it would fit.

"Christ yes," he whispered.

She licked him again, her tongue whirling slowly over the head. In the low light of the brace of candles and the crackling fire, she could see a drop leaking from his tip. Curious, she licked it up. She liked the way he tasted. Liked everything about this. Liked the way he watched her, his gaze hooded, his eyes dark. Liked the pleasure she was giving him, the power to make this hardened rake feel as if she were debauching him.

She thought again of what *The Tale of Love* had said, and she sucked him into her mouth. His fingers sifted through her hair, and his hips jerked. He liked this.

"Fuck, Grace."

Yes, he liked this. Tentatively, she took more of him, sucking, and licking, moving in time to the subtle rolls of his hips. Listening for the sounds he made. The low sighs. The throaty rumbles. She sucked again, harder this time, bringing him into the back of her throat, and still there was so much more of his length. She could not fit it all, so she gripped the base of him with her hand as he had shown her.

He said wicked things.

Words she had never heard before.

She wanted to make him say them again.

Her boldness grew. She felt strangely powerful, on her knees before him, making him lose control. She became aware, for the first time, of how beautiful it was to give pleasure. Every bit as great and heady a gift as receiving it.

"No more, Grace, or I will spend in your mouth," he said, his voice little more than a guttural plea now.

But she was not finished. Instinctively, she exhaled through her nose, trying to bring him deeper into her throat. His reaction was instant and affirming. His fingers tightened in her hair. She moaned around him, her mouth full, her own desire throbbing between her legs.

There was something unbearably erotic about this moment. They were both fully clothed, and yet her lips were on the most sensitive part of him, just as his had been upon her the night before.

She was not going to stop until he reached his pinnacle.

"Grace," he warned.

Still, she would not budge from her position. Nor would she stop. The only surrender she wanted this night was his, and she was determined to have it. His breathing was growing more ragged, his hips jerking forward, seeking more of her. And she gave him more. She gave him everything.

Until he stiffened, and the rush of his release was on her tongue. She swallowed it down, loving the taste of him. Loving the moment.

Loving…

Him.

Dear God. Surely she did not love Rand. She scarcely knew him. He was a jaded rake. Her feigned betrothed. He was only using her to gain his precious Scottish estate from his grandmother. And after he was done, she would never see him again.

Wiping a hand over her mouth, she sat back on her heels, an unwanted realization washing over her. One she did not wish to even contemplate. No, she was not in love with him.

It was not possible.

The passion and thrill of the moment had overwhelmed her.

"My God, woman," he said, fastening the fall of his breeches and pulling her to her feet. "You will be my undoing."

She could say the same for him, she thought grimly.

"Come here," he said, his voice gentle.

The expression on his face was tender. Affectionate, even. He opened his arms to her.

And she went. She went with ease, laying her head against his broad chest, wrapping her arms around his lean waist. She pressed her ear over his pounding heart, inhaled deeply of his scent. He hugged her to him tightly and kissed her crown.

They remained that way for an indeterminate span of time, united in a way they had not been before. She unabashedly reveled in his heat, his strength, absorbing every bit of it and of him. He held her without an exchange of words or kisses and yet somehow imparted a world of feeling.

Tonight had moved him, she could not help but to feel, every bit as much as it had moved her. This thing between them—feigned betrothal, debauching bargain, *whatever* it was—had altered once more. There was more heart now, joining the heat.

She did not mistake the difference.

"Grace, love," he said at last into the heavy silence. "I think *you* have debauched *me* tonight."

She smiled into his chest. "I think perhaps we have both debauched each other."

And she thought, too, that he had ruined her. Oh, not in the traditional sense. No one had caught him sneaking into her chamber. Not another soul knew what they were about. But he had ruined her in a different way.

In the way that she could not fathom ever feeling for another man the way she had begun to feel for this one. This wicked rake. This man in her arms.

The man she was pretending she was going to marry.

The man who, much to her dismay, she was beginning to fear she very much wanted to marry in truth.

Chapter Ten

AS IT TURNED out, the only thing better than imagining Grace Winter's pretty pink pout wrapped around Rand's cock had been…

Grace Winter's *actual*, glorious pink pout—puffed and swollen from his kisses—wrapped around his cock.

The sight of her taking him down her throat, on her knees before him, her eyes closed as if in her own bliss, the breathy moans she had made, the way she had refused to stop until he had exploded, filling her mouth with his seed…now that was the stuff of legend.

Of absolute, fucking *legend.*

Rand was out of his mind over it still, even in the biting December cold the next morning, riding over the snow alongside Lord Ashley Rawdon and the Duke of Coventry. Hertford had been nowhere to be found this morning. Rand harbored a suspicion his friend was sneaking into Miss Eugie Winter's chamber, but since he too was prowling about the halls in the darkest hour of the night, slipping into his own betrothed's room, he did not dare say a word. And Warwick, his oldest and best friend, had fallen in love with Rand's sister and refused to leave Lydia's side.

Curse it all.

Meanwhile, he had known the single, most carnal, most delicious, most blissful experience of his life last night thanks to his innocent betrothed.

Perhaps not so innocent, he amended inwardly, and not his betrothed. But rather, his *feigned* betrothed, as she was so oft correcting him. And not nearly as innocent as she had been before she knew him, thanks to their sessions of debauchery.

Only two down and five more to go until Christmas Day.

How he would manage a third night of debauchery without losing what last shreds of his restraint remained was beyond him.

"What was that, Aylesford?" Lord Ashley's voice sliced into his thoughts. "Did you just say fucking legend?"

"He did," Coventry confirmed, ever pithy.

Oh, Christ. Had he said that aloud? This was further proof that he was going mad. He was losing his damned mind over an auburn-haired siren who had sucked his cock with more enthusiasm than any woman he had ever known. A beautiful, stubborn, outspoken, bold lady who liked to sketch and who smelled like an English garden and who had verdant eyes and a heart-shaped beauty mark on her throat…

Lord Ashley and Coventry were both looking at him expectantly.

A gust of unseasonably cold wind hit him square in the face, nearly taking his hat. He clamped a hand down on the brim, holding on to the reins with the other. "I said you are a fucking legend," he improvised, addressing Lord Ashley.

Because everyone knew damned well his older brother, the Duke of Coventry, was as quiet as a mouse. Painfully shy. Likely a virgin himself. An odd gentleman, it was certain. Rand had no doubt Lord Ashley's presence at this house party was due to his brother needing the aid when it came to courting.

Devilishly hard to find a betrothed when one did not even speak to the fairer sex.

"Ah, but am I a *fucking* legend or a fucking *legend*?" Lord Ashley quipped with a broad grin. "That is the question."

Everyone also knew Lord Ashley was a scoundrel. His reputation was even worse than Rand's.

"Is it true that you tupped an opera singer, an actress, and a nun all at once?" he asked, giving voice to the old rumor in an effort to distract himself from the wayward bent of his thoughts.

Namely, Grace Winter.

"Not true at all," Lord Ashley said, his grin deepening. "The actress in question had been playing the role of a nun in her latest play. The opera singer did not resemble a nun in the slightest."

Rand had never bedded two women at once. Bedding one kept him more than occupied. And deuce it, now that he had a betrothed, he could not fathom the notion of bedding another woman at all.

Ever.

How sobering.

How bloody *alarming*.

"Ash," chided Coventry. "We discussed this."

"Ah, how could I forget?" Lord Ashley cast a derisive glance toward his brother the duke, his tone turning bitter. "I am to hide my past lest it muddy the waters for brother dearest as he attempts to find himself a bride. Familial obligations and all that rot."

"Bugbears," Coventry said. "I am yours. You are mine."

"Bugbears indeed," Rand grumbled. For he had more than a few of his own.

In fact, he had one in particular.

"Poor Gill has no choice but to wed because he inherited," Lord Ashley informed Rand. "Our father was a reckless wastrel. Could not be trusted with a ha'penny. Now Gill gets to pay the price. However, he is not particularly known for his ability to woo the fairer sex."

That was rather putting it nicely, if plainly, Rand thought. The Duke of Coventry was more painfully shy than a lady fresh from the schoolroom.

"You are his rearguard, as it were," Rand suggested.

"Precisely," Lord Ashley said. "Brilliant, Aylesford. I am my brother's romantic rearguard. I save his army from impending doom. Particularly, Miss Christabella Winter."

"Miss Winter is assisting me," Coventry bit out.

"She is the wrong Miss Winter," Lord Ashley argued with his brother. "You said you wish to marry Miss Prudence, did you not? She is the eldest and the loveliest of all the Winter sisters. Miss Christabella cannot compare. If you would simply cease spending all your time being distracted by the hellion and instead woo the woman you are meant to wed, your chance of success would increase immeasurably. Before someone else takes your place."

"Here now," Rand felt compelled to intervene. "I would argue Miss Grace is the loveliest of all the Winters by far. With her auburn hair and flashing green eyes, not to mention her perfect pink lips…"

He trailed off when he realized Lord Ashley and Coventry were both staring at him. And then he cleared his throat, his ears going hot. *Sweet God*, he was not *flushing*. He was not. He refused to believe it.

"In love, are you, Aylesford?" Lord Ashley taunted, his lips twitching.

No. Absolutely not. Bloody hell, no. Not a chance. Not now, not ever.

"Love?" he repeated, scoffing. "Such an emotion is better suited to fools and naïve women who sigh over silly novels filled with drivel. Do you not think?"

"I believe love is possible," Coventry said.

"With Pru?" Lord Ashley demanded, his voice suddenly sharp.

"Pru?" his brother repeated, raising a brow.

"Miss Prudence Winter," Lord Ashley amended, making a great show of flicking a speck of imaginary lint from the sleeve of his greatcoat as he held the reins in a loose grasp with his left hand. "You know to whom I refer."

"I did not question whom but rather your familiarity," the duke said pointedly.

"Go to the devil," bit out Lord Ashley.

And then he spurred his mount into a gallop, taking off over the snow-covered valley stretching before them.

Puffs of white filled the air in his wake, and Rand steadied his mount before turning back to Coventry, who was watching his brother's rapidly disappearing form in the distance with a curious expression on his face.

"He is angry with me," the duke observed.

"So it would seem," Rand agreed, noncommittally.

"I think he has fallen in love with Miss Prudence," Coventry said.

Love, again?

"Love is a fable," he dismissed. "A fiction. It is something we tell ourselves to believe in to distract us from how horrid life truly is."

"You do not believe in it?" the duke asked him, surprise marking his tone.

"I believed in it once," he elaborated. "Long enough to watch my former betrothed in the arms of another man, a man I once counted as a friend."

Coventry whistled lowly. "Brutal."

"Yes," he agreed shortly. "It was. A lesson learned, and all that."

"But do you not think what happened was not the fault of love, but rather the fault of the lady?" Coventry persisted. "The problem is not that love does not exist, but that your love was misplaced."

By God.

He had never thought of it in such terms before.

He frowned at Coventry. For a painfully shy, awkward man who could scarcely string together a series of sentences, the duke was remarkably astute.

"I had never thought of it quite that way before, Coventry," he admitted in spite of himself.

"When you ponder them enough, even the biggest problems become small," the duke said.

Rand could not argue the point. Because he very much feared the Duke of Coventry was right. And that everything he had believed these last few years had been terribly, hopelessly wrong.

GRACE DID NOT particularly feel like making merry.

Her rapidly escalating bargain with Rand had left her feeling confused. She had no wish to play another game of Snapdragon or Hoodman Blind. Instead, she was in the orangery, far away from the rest of the revelers. Though the glass-roofed room was heated, the chill of the day and the wind gusting outside still necessitated the use of a wrap.

The orange trees did not appear to mind, their glossed leaves lush and full. Fat fruits hung from their branches. Pomegranates and hibiscus beckoned as well, together creating the illusion that one had been secreted to an exotic clime.

The entire chamber was, she thought with a weary sigh, symbolic of her feigned betrothal with Aylesford: tempting, decadent, and false. The orange trees would wither in one night of brutal cold beyond these walls. The hibiscus would shrivel. And beyond this enchanted setting, her betrothal would fall as well.

Because it was not real.

Oranges were not meant to withstand the Oxfordshire winter.

Nor was her betrothal with Rand meant to last.

But last night had changed everything for her. She was losing her heart to him. It was undeniable. She could see it quite plainly. The last thing she had ever wanted was to fall in love with a self-assured scoundrel like him. The last thing she had ever imagined was that she would want their feigned betrothal to be real. However, she had, and she did. Which meant the time to make a decision was upon her.

She had to take action, and fast, if she wanted to protect herself from further hurt. She had been thinking of nothing but what she must do all day long. From the time she had risen in the morning, jarred from a dream of Rand kissing her so sweetly, the knowledge had weighed heavily upon her heart. There was only one option left to her: she needed to end this between them.

End the feigned betrothal.

End the bargain.

End the nights of debauchery.

And so doing, she could only hope, end the incessant longing she felt for him.

A footfall behind her alerted her to the fact that she was no longer alone before the deep, delicious baritone she had come to know so well even spoke.

"Grace."

How was it that even her name uttered in his voice sent a pang of longing through her?

Steeling herself against her reaction to him, she turned about. He was so handsome, a tentative smile on his lips. Those dashing dark waves she loved to run her fingers through fell over his brow in true rakish fashion. His bright-blue eyes were hungry and warm as they burned into hers.

A great rush of desire swept through her, along with remembrance of the intimacies they had shared. Their wicked nights of mutual debauchery. His kisses. His tongue on her most sensitive flesh. The way he had tasted. The delicious thickness of him in her hand, in her mouth.

But no, she must not think of any of those things now. She must forget all about the way he made her feel.

"My lord," she greeted tentatively, dipping into a proper curtsy as she forced her wits to return.

"Surely there is no need for such formality between us," he said smoothly, offering her an elegant bow. "After all, we are betrothed."

"Not in truth," she could not help but to point out, unable to keep the bitterness from her voice.

She could only hope he would not take note.

"But our betrothal could last for quite some time, Grace." He was solemn as he studied her. "It may take weeks or even months to convince my grandmother to deign to give me Tyre Abbey."

How could she bear weeks of being in his presence? Of him courting her? Months were an impossibility. It had only been days, and already he had dismantled all her defenses, like an invading army storming the castle walls. And she did not fool herself either—it was not because of his disarming looks or his undeniable charm. Rather, it was because of something else, something far deeper and more dangerous.

He brought her to life. He made her feel as if she had finally found the purpose in her life she had been searching for. That purpose was love. Loving him. But how could she love him when he was a fickle-hearted rake who had lived his own life flitting from one woman to the next, loving no one since his heart had been wrecked?

She shivered then, and it had nothing to do with the chill in the air. "I fear I may not be able to last that long, keeping up such a deception. Indeed, my lord, I am glad you sought me out, for I am beginning to think this entire bargain of ours was a mistake."

"A mistake?" He closed the distance between them and drew her into his arms.

She went willingly, *Lord help her*, because she could. Because being wrapped in his warm, strong embrace felt like home.

And yet still, she knew she must hold firm to her path. "Yes, a mistake. The past few days with you have been lovely. I cannot say I have not enjoyed our feigned betrothal, but I fear the risk is no longer worth the reward."

He searched her gaze. "Has something happened? Has one of your sisters divulged our secret?"

She shook her head, tamping down the sadness rising within her like flood waters, with every intent to drown. "Nothing has happened, and nor have any of my sisters betrayed my confidence. It is merely that I have realized, at long last, what I want from my future."

His brows snapped together. "You have?"

"Yes," she insisted, for that much was not a lie. She could not tell him the truth, however. For it was too embarrassing.

"What is it you want?" he asked softly, his gaze plumbing the depths of hers in a way she did not like.

Not long ago, they had been strangers. But now, she feared he could see too much.

You, she longed to say. *Even if your sallies are awful and you know precisely how handsome you are. You, because you hold me in your arms as if I am precious to you. Because your kisses make my knees weak. Because you found your way into my heart, and now I will never be the same.*

"I want freedom," she said instead. "The ability to live my life as I see fit. Ending my betrothal with you will prove to my brother just how misguided his notion of seeing me married to a lord truly is. I will tell him how horridly ill-suited we were, and how miserable marriage to an arrogant nobleman will make me."

Rand said nothing for a beat, simply stared at her. "Are we, Grace?"

"Are we what?" she asked, misery swirling through her.

"Are we horridly ill-suited?" he elaborated.

She tilted her head, considering him. "Of course we are, my lord. You are a rake who does not believe in love after your last betrothed betrayed you. You are too handsome for your own good, and all too aware of your own charms. You will be a duke one day. And I am no lady. My father was a merchant. My brother is a merchant. I will never be a duchess, and neither am I a beauty. My greatest asset is my determination, which will see me through now as it has always done."

His jaw tightened. "You are a lady, Grace. And beautiful. So damn beautiful."

"You need not ply me with flattery, my lord," she said, resolute. "I have already made up my mind. I cannot be your feigned betrothed any longer. If you want to tell my brother about the book, I cannot stop you. All I can do is ask that you lay the blame solely upon my shoulders."

"I am not plying you with flattery, damn it," he bit out. His chiseled jaw and cheekbones seemed as if they had been carved from stone.

"I am sorry, Lord Aylesford," she told him, because she

was. Sorrier than he could ever know. "I cannot uphold this farce. The risk is too great for me."

"What can the risk be in being my betrothed?" he demanded, cupping her jaw.

"Our bargain," she said, flushing furiously, longing to nuzzle her cheek in his palm but narrowly resisting that weakness. "My brother already saw me coming in from the gardens the other night wearing your greatcoat. And we have gone well beyond those kisses in the moonlight now. The embraces and the…debauchery we have shared. I have allowed my curiosity to get the better of me, and it has led me astray. I cannot risk being ruined. I cannot marry you."

"Why the devil not?" His voice, like his question, was indignant.

Of course he would be indignant and disbelieving. He was the handsome heir to a dukedom with more rakish wiles—to borrow Christabella's words—than any one man ought to possess.

"Because I do not want to marry you," she forced herself to say. Another lie. "And because you do not want to marry me."

The last, much to her regret, was the ugly truth.

He was dallying with her.

And she had allowed it. Had reveled in it, even. But her heart could no more survive Viscount Aylesford than the pomegranates and the hibiscus could thrive in the snowy world beyond the leaden panes of glass in the orangery. Her heart, like this sumptuous vegetation, would wither. Shrivel to nothing more than a husk.

"Marrying was never part of our agreement from the first, Grace," he said. "What has changed? Is it because of what happened last night?"

"No," she hastened to say. "What happened was…I will

never forget it. Nor will I forget any of the time I have spent with you. Whenever I make a sketch in the book you gave me, I will remember you with great fondness."

"Fondness." His lip curled, as if the very notion appalled him.

She could have said love, but she had no wish to reveal that much of herself to him. He had already seen her body. To expose her heart…she did not dare take such a foolish risk. For this man was a rake. He did not love. He wooed. He seduced.

"Fondness," she repeated. "And gratitude. I will not forget you, Lord Aylesford."

She extricated herself from his embrace at last, because she dared not linger there, absorbing his heat, relishing the strength of his lean body. His hands fell to his sides. She stepped back. And they stared at each other in stony silence. Overhead, the gray sky opened. Instead of snowflakes, it unleashed a torrent of ice. The sound of the tiny ice balls bouncing off the domed glass were like a thousand pins dropping, all at once.

"You truly mean to end our agreement, Grace?" He raked his fingers through his dark, wavy locks.

She swallowed. "I must."

And then, before she said something she would forever regret, or before she lost her strength, she turned and fled. Grasping her skirts in both hands, she lifted her hem and ran. Ran from the orangery, from its promise of the forbidden.

From the man who had stolen his way into her heart.

No footsteps followed her. And she did not need to look over her shoulder to discover he had not even bothered to chase her. He was letting her go.

Chapter Eleven

RAND HAD NO intention of letting Grace Winter go.

But he had reached an important realization as he watched her fleeing him in the orangery. He had spent so many years seducing women for a night of pleasure, that he had no notion of how to woo the woman whose heart he intended to claim as his own. Winning a woman for the night—even for a few weeks or months—was easily done. Winning a woman for a lifetime, however, was not so quickly achieved.

And a lifetime with Grace was precisely what he was after. Even if the word made his heart skip a beat and his chest ache. Even if it filled him with a breath-stealing mixture of awe and fear.

He needed reinforcements. Which was why he had enlisted the aid of his good friend the Earl of Hertford and the Winter sisters. Hertford had assembled them for him in the writing room where he had come upon Grace with *The Tale of Love* that fateful day not so long ago.

It was fitting then, that he held the book in his hands now.

"Lord Aylesford," said Prudence, the eldest of the sisters. "You wished an audience."

She was Lord Ashley's long Meg, as it were, even if Lord Ashley was apparently securing her hand for his brother. What a deuced tangled web that was. Rand was happy to stay out of it.

He bowed formally to the sisters, aware he must win all four ladies to his side. He needed all the help he could buy, beg, or steal.

Begging seemed the option of the day.

He felt as if he were facing the Spanish Inquisition.

"Thank you for agreeing to meet with me here," he said.

"You are fortunate indeed Hertford vouches for you and that he is standing guard at the door," Prudence told him, her tone chilly. "I can only suppose this sudden meeting has something to do with Grace."

"It has everything to do with her." He cleared his throat, warming to his cause. "As you are all aware, I offered your sister a bargain in exchange for her pretending to be my betrothed."

"You offered her a bargain, did you?" Prudence's brow raised.

"Forced her into doing your bidding is a far more apt description," said Eugie with a dismissive sniff.

"You stole her book and browbeat her into feigning a betrothal with you," added Christabella.

"All to gain some silly estate," Bea, the youngest and the only blonde amongst them, concluded.

Yes, he rather had done all those things. And when they phrased it thus, he certainly did sound like a reprobate of the first order.

He winced. "In my own defense, I courted her for days, attempting to get her to see the wisdom of my mutually beneficial plan."

"Yet she denied you," Prudence pointed out, her expression stony.

"Of course she did," he admitted. "Your sister is devilishly stubborn."

"A man such as yourself is not accustomed to being told *no*, I would imagine," observed Eugie.

"Not in some time," he allowed. "Indeed, not since my last betrothed cried off after I found her in the arms of my close friend. I have been dedicating myself to the art of keeping my heart from getting dashed to bits ever since. I have busied myself with leading the life of a rake and resorting to nothing more consequential than meaningless exchanges of desire. Until I met your sister."

"Whilst I am sure we are all sorry to hear your former betrothed treated you so unkindly, I fail to see what it has to do with you forcing our sister into pretending to be your betrothed," Miss Beatrix Winter said.

"I caught her reading a bawdy book in this very room," he said, holding up the book in question. "This book, as it would happen. And yes, I took it from her. Yes, I shamelessly used it as leverage against her. But in my own defense, it was only because I wanted her, and only her. I thought, at first, that it was because she was a challenge. I realized, in no time at all, that it is because she is unlike any lady I have ever met before. It is because there is only one Grace Winter, and I need to have her in my life, for the rest of my life, as my wife."

All four sisters gaped at him, quite as if he had just begun stripping away his coat and breeches in their midst.

Prudence was the first to find her tongue. "You are saying you want to marry Grace in truth?"

"Yes." He stalked forward, *The Tale of Love* extended before him. "And you may have this book. I no longer have need of it. Though she refused to tell me which of you it belongs to, I can only gather it must be one or all of you."

Their expressions were identically guilty, confirming his suspicions.

Prudence took the book from him hastily and handed it off to the flame-haired sister, who tucked it neatly into a secret pocket which must have been sewn into the skirt of her gown for just such a purpose.

Clever minxes.

No gentleman stood a chance against them.

"I am in love with your sister," he announced.

There. He had said it. Admitted it aloud. Given voice to the emotions he had spent the last few days trying his damnedest to ignore.

"Truly in love with her?" Eugie asked, her eyes narrowing upon him.

"So in love with her, it terrifies me," he said, unashamed. "So in love with her, I cannot bear the notion of her ending our betrothal."

Prudence's brows rose. "Grace has decided to end the betrothal? What have you done, you scoundrel? Did you hurt her?"

Bloody hell, what did they take him for?

"Of course I did not hurt her," he snapped. "Have you not heard a word I just said? I am in love with her, and I want to make her my wife. But she has decided she must have her freedom or some such rot. She said continuing our farce was too great a risk, and that she was going to tell your brother herself about *The Tale of Love*."

"She cannot tell Dev about *the book*," protested Miss Christabella Winter. "He will stop at nothing until he confiscates the entire set from us."

"You have more than just the one?" he asked, shocked in spite of himself. He supposed he ought to have learned by now just how resourceful and bold the Winter sisters were.

"We have them all," said Miss Christabella, her tone smug.

Lord help the man who chose to wed *that* Winter sister, he thought.

"But that is neither here nor there," interrupted Prudence. "Freedom is not rot, Lord Aylesford. Not if that is what she truly wants."

"I would give her freedom as my wife," he countered. "And my love. And whatever else she wants. Forever."

"But will you be true to her?" asked Miss Eugie Winter. "Your reputation is not particularly promising, my lord."

He met Eugie's gaze, unflinching, for this was a question he had no trouble answering. "I will be true to her until my last breath. I want no other."

"A reformed rake," Miss Christabella said with a sigh, holding a hand over her heart.

"A man," he said, "who is in love. That is all."

The way he felt for Grace eclipsed the way he had ever felt for another. The love he'd believed he had for Georgina could not even compare. A wife had been the last thing he had wanted when he arrived in Oxfordshire, and now, he could not fathom anything but making Grace his forever.

He admired her wit, her resilience, her boldness. He appreciated her beauty, her giving nature. The bond she shared with her sisters, the impishness that led to her seeking out *The Tale of Love*, the natural sensuality she embraced.

All of it, and all of her, he loved.

"I believe he is telling the truth," said Miss Beatrix, her tone solemn.

"Of course I am telling the truth," he bit out. "Why else would I humble myself before you? She has told me she is intent upon ending our betrothal, but I am equally intent upon stopping her and making her see reason."

"How is your confession to us going to help with that?" Miss Prudence queried coolly.

"Because I need your help," he admitted. "I need you to tell me what I must do to win her heart."

HER SISTERS WERE behaving strangely, and Grace knew it. All four of them descended upon her chamber that afternoon, interrupting her solitude and misery both. She opened the door at the strident knock, half expecting and half hoping to find Rand there on the threshold, his handsome face etched with determination and wicked intent to seduce, to find the four of them standing shoulder to shoulder in the hall, rather reminiscent of a battle formation.

"Are you ill?" Pru demanded, taking stock—no doubt—of her red, watery eyes and puffy nose.

"I think I may have developed the ague," she lied, sniffling.

"You look wretched," Christabella observed, her tone sympathetic.

"Why are you hiding?" Eugie asked.

"Do you feel as if you are feverish?" Bea prodded, the only one amongst them to evince even a hint of proper concern.

"Why are all four of you here at once?" she asked, suspicion slicing through her.

"We came to check upon you, of course," Pru said, her tone even and neat. Laden with reason.

"Lady Emilia asked us to," added Eugie.

"Your absence has been noted," confirmed Christabella.

"Your cheeks do not appear flushed, nor do your eyes look glazed, as if you are feverish," noted Bea, who found great purpose in science and medicine.

On a sigh, Grace stepped back, gesturing for her sisters to enter her chamber. "You may as well come in, all of you.

There is no sense in you lingering in the hall."

All four of her sisters bustled into the chamber, and Grace closed the door behind them before turning to face them at once.

"Well?" she demanded. "What is the reason for you coming here in the midst of the afternoon? I should think one lady attempting to take a nap is hardly of note."

"Of course not," Pru agreed shrewdly, "but you do not look as if you were napping, darling."

"You look as if you were sobbing," added Christabella.

"Is there a reason you are upset?" Bea asked.

"Or is there perhaps a gentleman in particular who has upset you?" Eugie prodded.

Her heart was broken. She had fallen in love with a man who would never love her back. She had engaged in acts with him that were too wicked to speak aloud. And then she had told him she could not bear to continue with their feigned betrothal, and he had not even bothered to stay her with a protest.

Likely, he had already found another feigned betrothed in the hours since she had last seen him. The arrogant, handsome devil would have no trouble, she was sure, finding her replacement.

Most hurtful of all was the realization that everything they had shared had been commonplace to him. No more special than a breath or a step he took. While for her, their every kiss, touch, interaction had been *everything*.

"Grace?" Pru asked, her tone gentling. "Are you well?"

She inhaled, trying to calm herself. Trying to stave off the rising tide of misery. But the hurt was too great. It was devastating. The grief threatened to consume her.

"I," she began, only to falter as a sob stole the rest of her words.

Tears were running down her cheeks before she could stifle them.

At once, her sisters gathered around her, taking her in an embrace from all sides until she was in the middle, and their arms were banded in an unbreakable circle around her.

"Tell us, Grace," said Bea.

"If Aylesford hurt you, I will break his arm," Eugie vowed.

"I will punch him in the eye," Christabella offered. "He will not look nearly so pretty with a bruise."

"If he hurt you, *we* will hurt *him*," said Pru calmly. "You must tell us, Grace. What has you so upset?"

"I am in love with him," she managed to admit, in spite of the sobs clogging her throat and in spite of her own embarrassment. "I am in love with a man who does not want to marry me, who is a rakish thief of hearts and books, who only wanted to pretend to be betrothed so he could gain an estate in Scotland. I am in love with a man who shall never love me back. Dear God, I am the greatest fool who ever lived."

"Certainly not the greatest fool, darling," said Pru, patting her back. "That title has been reserved for another far more deserving soul. Come, let us go for a walk, shall we?"

"A walk?" She frowned at her sisters. "Looking as I do? I cannot bear it."

"You can and you shall," Christabella told her softly. "Trust us, Grace."

"You shan't be sorry," Bea added.

"You are in love with Lord Aylesford?" Eugie probed. "Truly?"

"Truly," she said, her misery complete. "I know how foolish and ludicrous it sounds. That is why I have been hiding in my chamber. I have ended our feigned betrothal. I have yet to muster up the daring to tell Dev, because he caught us alone in the gardens the other night…"

"Come with us, if you please, Grace," Pru insisted. "We have just the thing to lighten your mood."

IT WAS DEVILISHLY close to dinner by the time Rand had procured each of the necessary items the sisters had assured him would please Grace. The scratches on his cheek were still smarting. The cursed fat cat he had wrangled from the stables was stalking somewhere about the salon—likely lurking beneath a settee, plotting her next attack.

The pear tartlets were arranged nicely on a china plate. He also had, at the ready, a set of watercolors he had easily coaxed his sister into forfeiting—Lyd preferred science to art, always. He had managed to thieve some hibiscus blossoms from the orangery. And, he had written her a poem.

The poem was abysmal.

The angry, fat cat was old and disagreeable.

The pear tartlets were remnants from dinner the night before.

The watercolors had been used.

But he had done his best to acquire all the items the Winter sisters had assured him would please Grace and aid in his attempts to woo her. He had never even courted a lady since Georgina. There had been no need. And now that he wanted to do things the right way, the proper way, he found himself unaccountably nervous.

What if the sisters would not fetch Grace as they had promised they would?

What if Grace refused to see him?

What if he could not change her mind with wooing?

Worst of all, what if she could never return his love? If she would not marry him?

He could not bear to contemplate such an unbearable notion. He had to believe he could win her heart. The passion between them was real and undeniable. Surely, they could build upon that. Even if she did not harbor tender feelings for him, certainly the pleasure they shared could grow and blossom and deepen over time.

Could it not?

He was spared from further tortured musings when the door to the salon opened and there was Grace on the threshold. Her eyes were puffy and rimmed with pink. Her nose was as red as a holly berry. She looked as if she had spent the last few hours weeping.

And even with her rumpled gown, auburn ringlets worn loose from her coiffure to frame her face, her countenance pale, her mouth drawn, she was the most beautiful woman he had ever beheld. She was beloved to him. The only woman he wanted.

Forever.

It was a word that would have sent him fleeing not long ago. Before he had met Grace, he had never even contemplated the thought of marrying again in truth. He had simply been so consumed in his life of endless, meaningless pleasure. His thoughts had been for gaining Tyre Abbey and for little else.

But she had changed all that.

She had changed *him.*

And she had most definitely changed his heart, for she owned it now. It was hers, and hers alone.

"Lord Aylesford," she said, her tone shocked.

He wished she had called him Rand, but there was no hope for that.

He was treated to the vague glimpse of four sisters' faces in the hall behind her before the door closed at her back, leaving them alone.

"Grace," he greeted, bowing.

She dipped into an abbreviated curtsy but did not smile. "What is this about? You have somehow cozened my sisters into aiding you with this feigned betrothal nonsense? Are you holding the book over their heads as well? I have told you already that I will claim it. It is mine, and mine alone. The blame must be laid solely upon me. Go to my brother as you must, but I alone am the guilty one."

"This is not about the book, Grace," he told her, striding forward. Closing the distance between them because he had to. Because he could not bear to be so near to her, and yet unable to touch her.

But she shied away from him, flitting to the periphery of the salon as if she were a butterfly chased from a blossom. "What is it about then, Lord Aylesford? Why must you insist upon plaguing me? I have already told you I am done with this feigned betrothal. I want no more of it."

"That is perfectly fine by me," he told her, stalking to where she stood. "I do not want a feigned betrothal with you either."

Her brow furrowed. And *Christ*, it was adorable.

"You do not?" she asked.

"No," he said. "I do not. I want a real betrothal."

She stiffened, her chin tipping up. "I wish you and whatever lady you have chosen well, in that case. I am sure she will make a lovely duchess one day."

"Yes, she will." He moved closer still. Until he was near enough to touch her. "No other lady could possibly be as perfect as she."

"Finding a replacement did not take you long, did it?"

She laughed, but he did not miss the bitterness hidden within her levity, and it gave him hope. "Several hours, and she is such a paragon that you have already decided you will make her your wife in deed rather than your feigned betrothed. How fortunate for you, my lord. You see? I did you a favor in setting you free of our odious bargain."

"You did do me a great favor," he said, sliding an arm around her waist and drawing her lush body against his. Lord, how perfect was her fit to him. How right. How wonderful. His cock sprang to life.

The scent of glorious summer blossoms and Grace hit him, directly in the heart.

"What are you doing, Aylesford?" She began to squirm, as if intent upon escaping his hold. "I cannot think your betrothed would appreciate your freedom with my person."

"Do *you* mind?" he asked pointedly, kissing the upturned tip of her nose.

Curse it, did he spot a few errant freckles there? How glorious. Why had he not noticed them before? And what other mysteries did she hold? He could not wait to unlock them all, one by one.

"Of course I mind, my lord." Her palms came to rest upon his chest, and she gave him a solid push. "I will not dally with you when you are intent upon marrying someone else. Have you not heard a word I have uttered to you, you arrogant jackanapes?"

"I rather think it is you who are not hearing me, my love," he told her, searching her gaze. "I do not want a feigned betrothal with you, Grace Winter, because I want our betrothal to be real. I want to marry you. *You* are the woman I have chosen. *You* are the only woman I want."

He paused then, pondering what she had just said to him. "Even if you do think me an arrogant jackanapes," he added.

She went still, all the fight seeming to drain from her. Her green eyes were wide, searching his frantically, as if seeking the slightest hint of deceit. But she could look all she liked, for she would find none.

"You want to marry *me*?" she asked. "In truth?"

"You," he said, grinning. "To hell with the feigned betrothal. You are the one for me, Grace. I have realized something profound during my presence here. For so long, I believed love did not exist. But in fact, my love was misplaced. All along, I was waiting for the right woman to come into my life."

"The right woman," she repeated, sounding dazed.

"The perfect woman," he agreed. "Perfect for me in every way. You are the only lady of my acquaintance who has looked down her nose at me. The only one who ever dared to put me in my place."

"Anyone could have corrected your high opinion of yourself," she said swiftly. "That alone is not reason for marriage."

"Is love?" he asked.

"Love?" she repeated, such longing in her voice, it nearly broke him then and there.

"Yes," he persisted, past the lump in his throat. "Love. I love you, Grace Winter, and you are the woman I want to marry. A feigned betrothal with you cannot be enough, because only a real betrothal will do. I aim to make you mine. To keep you mine. Will you be mine, my love? Now and forever?"

Her lips parted. For the second time since he had first met her, he was so desperate for a yes from her he could practically taste it.

Instead, all he heard was an ear-splitting yowling, emerging from somewhere in the chamber.

Christ.

The fat cat.

Her brows snapped together, her expression fast changing into one of befuddlement. "What was that wretched sound?"

For a beat, he felt as if he had returned to that enchanted night in the gardens when she had caught him smoking a cigar and she had asked him what the wretched smell was.

"Your cat," he told her, wincing when the yowl turned into a howl.

What the devil was the matter with the creature?

She blinked, looking more befuddled than ever. "I do not have a cat."

"Correction," he told her, trying to make the best of his admittedly lackluster attempt at procuring her the feline she had always longed for, according to her sisters. "You *did* not have a cat before. But you *do* have one now, just as you have so desperately wanted."

Grace frowned. "I never wanted a cat. When I was a girl, a cat I rescued from the streets scratched me horribly, and I have not trusted felines since."

He frowned right back at her as another terrible meow filled the chamber. "But your sisters…"

Her sisters had led him on a merry chase, he was beginning to realize.

Troublesome minxes, every last one of them.

"My sisters told you I wanted a cat?" she asked. "Why would they do that?"

"I am afraid I am beginning to suspect their purposes were nefarious," he said grimly. "May I also suppose you do not like pear tartlets, watercolors, or poetry?"

Her lips twitched. "Good heavens. Did you truly acquire a demonic cat, pear tartlets, watercolors, and poetry just for me?"

"The cat is not demonic," he argued as another yowl tore

through the chamber. "Aggrieved would be a better choice of words. Apparently, the little lass prefers her bed in the stables to this salon, though I cannot fathom why."

Grace's fingertips caressed his cheek lightly.

He was so starved for her touch that his reaction was instant. Blistering. His cock went stiff, and he caught her wrist, holding her in a gentle grip while he pressed a kiss to her palm.

"Did the aggrieved cat do this to you?" she asked.

"Trundling the creature from the stables to this chamber was no easy feat," he said, rather than admit he had been bested by a feline.

He would do it all over again. Anything to convince her how serious he was about spending the rest of his life with her. He would even allow her vexing sisters to make a fool of him once more.

"Oh, Rand," she said. "I cannot believe you did this."

"You cannot believe I amassed a whole lot of things you do not like?" He raised his brows, aiming for comical effect. "I am afraid I have mucked this up quite badly by seeking the counsel of your sisters. I should have simply told you what I felt for you in the orangery. I would have, but I was too bloody scared."

"I was scared too," she told him. "That is why I ended it between us. Because I knew I could not bear to continue spending time with you, pretending to be your betrothed, all while falling more in love with you each day. I had to put an end to it to protect my heart."

This was promising indeed.

He swallowed down a knot of emotion. "You are in love with me?"

Her smile was tremulous. "Yes. Somehow, I lost my heart to an arrogant scoundrel who coerced me into being his feigned betrothed. Who stole my book…"

"I returned it to your sisters," he told her. "Your secret is safe. I was an utter cad for using it against you. Can you forgive me, my love?"

The cat made another low, keening sound.

"Of course, I forgive you." She searched his gaze. "Do you truly mean it, that you love me?"

"Would I have brought you a demonic cat if I did not?" he quipped.

"I am still right about your sallies," she told him solemnly. "Say it again, Rand. Tell me again."

That was easy. The words left him, unfettered and true.

"I love you, Grace Winter."

"Oh," she said. Tears glistened in her dark-green eyes. "I love you too."

"Thank Christ," he hissed, dipping his head until their foreheads touched. "I am settling upon the favor you owe me from our debauchery bargain. Tell me you will marry me."

"You are not doing this because of the estate, are you?" she asked then.

"I do not want Tyre Abbey," he told her. "I thought I did. I thought securing the estate would fulfill me, but I realized something far more profound along the way. All I want is *you*."

"All I want is you, too," she whispered.

Gratitude washed over him, along with the sweetest relief. And love. So damned much love.

He took her mouth with his at last, and there was little skill in this kiss. It was raw and ardent and real. A promise. He devoured her lips, and when she sucked his tongue into her mouth, he could not stifle his moan of appreciation. The kiss deepened, until they were clutching each other desperately.

Until the low, throaty meows of the fat cat intruded.

He tore his mouth from hers with great reluctance, unable to keep the stupid grin of happiness from his lips. "I hate to stop kissing you, darling, but the demonic cat sounds as if it is in pain."

Grace smiled back at him. "Where is the poor creature?"

"Beneath a settee, I believe," he grumbled, inwardly cursing the thing.

If it weren't for the beast, he would still be kissing the woman he loved. Instead, he took her by the hand and led her in the direction of the dreadful sounds. They reached a gilt-framed settee, and he jabbed his finger unceremoniously toward the cushion.

Before he could protest, Grace grasped her skirts and sank to her knees.

And for the second time in their acquaintance, her rump was beckoning to him as she poked about beneath a piece of furniture. As tempting as the sight was—and as much as he appreciated it—he had no wish for the cat to attack her.

"Grace," he protested. "Leave the thing alone. I will enlist a footman to help me remove it."

"You will do nothing of the sort," she said, her voice muffled. "There you are, you little darling. How sweet."

Frowning, he dropped to his knees alongside her, and when he looked beneath the settee, he saw the reason for the yowling and his betrothed's sudden cooing both.

The fat cat had given birth to four squirming, wet kittens.

"This certainly explains her outrage," he said softly.

"She is not demonic at all," Grace told him, casting him a glance that melted his heart. "She is a mama. Oh, Rand. Aren't they adorable?"

He was sure they were, but at the moment, he only had eyes for her. "When can I marry you, Grace?"

He wanted to marry her now. This moment. He never

wanted to let her go. When he had watched her fleeing from him in the orangery, it had torn him apart.

"Soon," she said softly. "Rand?"

"Yes, Grace love?"

"Kiss me," she ordered him.

He did not waste a moment in closing the distance between them and pressing his lips to hers as happiness and love blossomed inside him.

To the devil with feigned betrothals. He had what was real and what was right and *all* he needed. Now, and forever.

Epilogue

"WHILE YOUR OFFER is tempting, I must regretfully decline, my lord," Grace told her new husband with a teasing smile, intentionally echoing the words she had said to him not long ago, when she had initially turned down his feigned betrothal.

"One more?" he prodded with a wicked smile that did untold things to her insides, holding a savoy biscuit to her lips.

"Perhaps just one," she allowed, and then took a ladylike bite from the airy biscuit.

It was delicious, and there was no denying it. But not nearly as delicious as the man before her. With his dark, tousled hair and those bright-blue eyes of his burning into hers, not even the most decadent dessert could distract her from what she wanted most.

Him.

They had married at a small affair in the country attended by her family and his. After a lengthy breakfast presided over by his grandmother, the august dowager Duchess of Revelstoke—during which Grace had earned her reluctant approval—they had departed for one of the lesser Revelstoke estates.

Rand had prepared for their arrival in true fashion. There had been a steaming bath awaiting her, along with a plate of savoy biscuits, and tea just the way she liked. All five of their cats had accompanied them for the journey, as both Grace and Rand had gotten quite attached to the mama cat—now named Snowflake—and her litter of adorable kittens.

In all, though the winter was cold, their travel had been onerous, and the day had been long, Grace had never been happier.

"Another bite, Lady Aylesford?" Rand asked, the half-eaten biscuit still in his long, elegant fingers.

She shook her head. "All I want now is my husband, Lord Aylesford."

A glint she recognized all too well had entered his hooded gaze. "Truly? I thought you preferred blond gentlemen with brown eyes. And that I was in need of some fortifying pie."

Of course, he had not forgotten her merciless teasing of him.

She bit her lip. "I must admit, I still treasure the expression on your face when I said that to this day."

"That is because you are a wicked minx, Lady Aylesford." His grin deepened, until he was smoldering with sensual intent. He placed the biscuit upon the plate before taking her into his arms. "Fortunately for you, I am wicked too."

She wound her arms around his neck. They were both clad in nothing more than dressing gowns. Her hair was damp from her bath, and his was too, the long ends tickling her fingertips.

"I think it is time for our debauchery bargain to begin anew," she murmured.

"Bloody hell, I love you," he said.

And then, his mouth was on hers, before she could even tell him that she loved him, too. But it did not matter, because he was kissing her with such fervor, her capacity for thought fled. Because this was the moment she had been waiting for all through their betrothal.

The moment she had been waiting for, it seemed, since that first kiss in the moonlit gardens back at Abingdon Hall.

His tongue was in her mouth. Their hands were everywhere, caressing through the barrier of their silken robes. Fingers finding knotted belts and plucking them open. All the obstacles between them fell away. Their kiss deepened, becoming ravenous. Laden with promise.

They fell onto the bed together, their mouths fused. His body was hot and hard against hers, and it turned the ache between her thighs into a steady throb. She knew what she wanted, and it was him inside her.

But it would seem her rakish husband was determined to torment her, because he was in no hurry. He left her lips to trail a series of kisses across her jaw to her ear.

"I love you, Grace," he whispered. "So very much."

"I love you," she said, so eager for him she could not keep herself from arching her back and thrusting her breasts into his chest.

Her nipples were already taut, eager buds, but the light abrasion of his chest hair against them coupled with his warm strength was enough to make her even wilder for him. And then he licked her ear and caught it between his teeth, and a wild torrent of desire ran down her spine.

She could already feel the evidence of her need for him pooling between her thighs. His knowing fingers parted her there, dipping into her folds.

"Mmm," he rumbled into her ear. "You are dripping for me, love."

He found the most responsive part of her, the bundle of need that never ceased pulsing in his presence, and worked his fingertips over it in slow, maddening circles. Her hips jerked from the bed in response. She was coming undone for him with such ease.

She thought he could make her spend with a single look.

He licked behind her ear as he worked her flesh, rubbing harder. The desire inside her tightened. She felt as if she were drawn taut. As if at any moment, she would lose herself. These past few weeks of waiting and wanting had turned her into a wild woman. And there was only one cure for what ailed her.

"I want you inside me, Rand," she said, running her nails lightly down his back.

He felt so good. Too good. As if every part of him had been fashioned just for her.

"Damn it, I am trying to be a gentleman," he growled, kissing his way down her throat, lingering on a particular patch of flesh. "This heart-shaped mark haunts me in my dreams."

"I do not want you to be a gentleman," she urged. "And the heart-shaped mark, like all of me, is yours now. Yours to take. Yours to claim."

With another low rumble of approval, he made his way to her breasts. He was still working his fingers over her in seductive strokes that brought her nearer and nearer to oblivion. Each rotation brought her closer to the abyss. When he sucked a nipple into the wet heat of his mouth, she was lost.

Her release was sudden and powerful, bursting like a fireworks display in the night sky. Brilliant and beautiful and breathtaking. He bit her nipple lightly, then moved to her other breast, flicking his tongue over the peak.

Ripples of pleasure were still rolling through her by the time he kissed a path of fire down her belly and settled between her thighs. She offered no protest this time, knowing there was no more decadent pleasure to be had than this man's mouth and tongue upon her. She spread her legs wider, her fingers slipping into his hair. The first touch of his tongue, one long lick up her slit, was so wondrous, she could not stifle her own moan of approval.

He licked over her engorged bud, alternating between quick little lashes of his tongue and long, slow flutters. White-hot desire rocketed through her. Already, she was close to spending again. He buried his face deeper in her sex, an answering moan rumbling from him. He consumed her as if she were a feast. As if he were a starving man.

There was no more erotic sight than that dark head bent between her thighs, intent upon giving her pleasure. She lost control once more. This time, her spend was faster, more potent than the last. She was still shuddering beneath him when he rose, positioning his cock against her throbbing entrance.

"Are you ready, love?" he asked, his breathing ragged and harsh. "I have to be inside you now."

"Yes." She moved her hips urgently, seeking him. "I have been ready for you forever."

And indeed, it seemed to her that she had.

His beautiful face was a study in restraint as he rocked against her. Just the tip of him entered her at first. The sensation was exquisite. She was stretched, aching, and hungry in a new way. But he was going so slowly. And she was impatient. Grace moved, rocking her hips, bringing him deeper. There was a stinging burn as her body adjusted to him. A pinch.

"Damn it, woman, I am trying to make this as painless as possible for you," he said.

"Then get inside me, now," she ordered him, breathless.

Her words seemed to be all the impetus he required. He started moving faster, thrusting deeper. He guided her legs around his waist, and he reached a part of her that she had not even known existed. If she had thought the sensation of him inside her had been exquisite before, he proved her wrong now.

It was magnificent.

Glorious.

Thrilling.

"How does this feel?" he asked her, his voice tense, the cords in his neck standing in rigid relief.

"Wonderful," she said, her back bowing from the bed as she tried to bring him deeper, seeking out the delicious friction of him sliding in and out of her. "I want more."

He chuckled and then pressed a kiss to her lips. "Easy, darling. I have no wish to cause you pain."

Her arms were back around his neck, and she was hanging on to him. "Make love to me, Rand."

On a growl, he began a new rhythm, sliding in and out of her, making the desire within her build to a new crescendo all over again. He withdrew almost completely, then sank inside her, repeating it until she was mindless and boneless beneath him. And when he reached between them to stroke her pearl, it was more than she could take. Desire overtook her. Quaked through her. She cried out, her body tightening on his, as the most primal wave of bliss burst over her.

He continued pumping into her, his mouth on hers. And then suddenly, his big body stiffened. He threw his head back and cried out as the hot flood of his release emptied within her. When it was over, he collapsed against her, their hearts pounding as one.

They remained thus, locked tightly in each other's arms, for an indeterminate span of time. And all Grace could think of was how much she loved him. Of how thankful she was for the day she had agreed to become a wicked rakehell's feigned betrothed. She could never have imagined it would turn out like this. That she would find the man she was meant to love forever in him.

But she had, and she was Rand's now. Just as he was hers.

At last, he disengaged from her, seemingly as reluctant to put an end to their closeness as she was. He rolled to his side, pulling her across his bare chest as he did so. She sprawled against him happily, her head over his hammering heart.

She tangled her fingers through his where they rested on his taut abdomen and tilted her head back so she could see his face.

"I think that perhaps I do not prefer blond-haired, brown-eyed gentlemen after all," she told him with a soft smile.

"Good," he said, grinning right back at her and giving their entangled fingers a squeeze. "Because I find that I prefer willful auburn-haired ladies who tell me I need to eat pie."

"You are fortunate indeed, Lord Aylesford," she teased. "Because I believe I fit that description perfectly."

"Yes, I am, Lady Aylesford," he agreed, devotion smoldering in his gaze, "and yes, you do. And I love you so."

"I love you more," she said.

Then she drew his lips to hers for another kiss, and neither of them said a word more for quite some time.

THE END.

Dear Reader,

Thank you for reading *Willful in Winter*! I hope you enjoyed this fourth book in my The Wicked Winters series and that Grace and Rand's story gave you all the feels, with a side of laughter and steam. Writing each of the stories in this series has been a true joy for me, and I am so thankful to you, my wonderful readers, for embracing this series. I hope Grace and Rand brightened your day!

As always, please consider leaving an honest review of *Willful in Winter.* Reviews are greatly appreciated! If you'd like to keep up to date with my latest releases and series news, sign up for my newsletter here or follow me on Amazon or BookBub. Join my reader's group on Facebook for bonus content, early excerpts, giveaways, and more.

If you'd like a preview of *Wagered in Winter*, Book Five in The Wicked Winters, featuring Lord Ashley Rawdon who is supposed to be convincing Pru to marry his brother, but ends up falling for her himself, do read on.

Until next time,

Scarlett

Wagered in Winter

By
Scarlett Scott

Lord Ashley Rawdon has agreed to accompany his painfully shy brother, the Duke of Coventry, to a country house party with the goal of securing him a wealthy bride. A dedicated rake, Ashley is so confident he can help his brother to ensnare the lady of his choosing, he offers him a wager. It's too bad the lady his brother selects is Miss Prudence Winter, who is infuriating, stubborn, and far too alluring.

Pru has no patience for sophisticated, handsome scoundrels like Lord Ashley. Nor does she seek a husband. All she wants is to spend the house party in peace so she can return to her charity work in London. But Lord Ashley is persistent. And far too charming.

Ashley's plan is proceeding splendidly. Until he finds himself alone with Pru, and he cannot resist stealing a kiss…

Chapter One

Oxfordshire, 1813

LORD ASHLEY RAWDON had a problem.

A tall, beautiful, brunette problem.

Ordinarily, such an obstacle would be pleasant for a man who had devoted his life to chasing, wooing, and pleasing the fairer sex. But in this situation, he was not chasing, wooing, and attempting to win the lady in question for himself.

Rather, he was attempting to do so for his brother.

There would be no delicious culmination of his efforts. He would not be taking the lovely Miss Prudence Winter's supple berry-colored lips with his. He would never help her out of her gown or find his way beneath her petticoats, and he most certainly would not know the delight of spreading her legs and plying his tongue to her cunny until she spent.

Damn and blast.

Gill was going to owe him after this.

Ash followed Miss Prudence Winter down the massive hall of Abingdon House at a discreet distance. He had no wish to cause a scandal and find himself forced into marrying the chit, after all. Even if he had always had a secret yearning for long Megs like her. And even if he found her delectably tempting.

He put the last down to his forced rustication at a country house party all in the name of helping his painfully shy brother, the Duke of Coventry, obtain a bride. Namely, one Miss Prudence Winter. She was the eldest of all the Winter sisters, wealthy ladies who hailed from trade and whose brother Devereaux Winter was doing his damnedest to use his newfound connection to nobility to ensnare aristocratic husbands for his sisters.

Hence the advent of this blasted party at Christmastide.

Hence Ash's presence in Oxfordshire.

And his current plight.

Miss Prudence disappeared into a chamber four doors down, and Ashley sped up his strides, casting a cautionary glance over his shoulder, before he, too, crossed the threshold and joined her. He found himself inside the sprawling, two-story library of Abingdon House.

Alone with the woman his brother wanted to make his future duchess.

He closed the door at his back and cleared his throat to make himself known.

Pressing a hand to her heart, Miss Prudence Winter spun about, her skirts whirling around her ankles. He fancied he caught a glimpse of slim, stocking-clad perfection and the hint of appealingly curved calves.

"What are you doing in here, my lord?" she demanded, frowning at him.

Even her displeasure was somehow alluring.

He ground his molars and forced himself to imagine a shovel's worth of cold December snow being dumped down the fall of his breeches. Anything to abate the irritating desire the disapproving creature glowering at him now inspired.

"Forgive me, Miss Winter," he said, bowing stiffly. "I find myself bored and in search of diversion. I had not realized the library was occupied."

Her lips pursed, and she raised a dark brow high, her

countenance making it apparent she did not believe him. Nor was she wrong to find him or his motives suspect. A wise woman, Miss Prudence Winter.

"Now that you realized I am within, you can see the necessity for you to go," she told him coolly.

Here was the other thing about her. Unlike most females of his acquaintance, Miss Winter was not easily won over by him. Upon their every previous interaction—three, not that he was counting—she had made him work for each word she deigned to utter.

"It would be wise for me to observe propriety and go," he agreed calmly. "However, now that I have your ear, I find myself loath to leave."

"Lord Ashley, you do not have my ear, you have my irritation," she countered, sweeping toward him with purpose in her step. "I have told you before that I have absolutely no tolerance for meaningless flattery."

Yes, she had, the impertinent baggage. Only worse.

"I believe you said you had no tolerance for meaningless flattery from empty-headed rakehells," he mused, stroking his jaw as if in deep thought.

There was no need for thought. She had said precisely that. Verbatim.

"Then one wonders why you have followed me here, Lord Ashley," she countered, standing near enough now that he could touch her if he wished.

Of course, he wished.

He clenched his fists to stave off the desire.

"I did not follow you, Miss Winter," he lied.

"Of course you did," she countered. "Just as you followed me on the two previous occasions our paths have crossed."

"Three occasions," he muttered below his breath before he could think better of it.

Ash could not be certain if she had truly forgotten how many times they had spoken or if she was intentionally nettling him. With Miss Prudence Winter, it could certainly be either.

"I beg your pardon?" she asked.

He cleared his throat again and then busied himself by brushing the sleeve of his coat. Affecting *ennui* was a special gift of his. "Nothing to concern yourself over, Miss Winter. I can assure you, I have not been following you."

She tilted her head, considering him with a chocolate-brown gaze he could not help but to feel saw far too much. "As it pleases you, Lord Ashley. Please just go. I am in search of a book to read. Surely there is some other lady in attendance you can attempt to seduce in my stead? I am certain I have made my lack of enthusiasm known."

Curse it, the woman was bold and brash. He would have told Gill to seek another bride, but the bind their wastrel father had left the estates in meant Gill needed to take a wife with the sort of immense funds only a Winter possessed. And the Winter sisters were all a troublesome lot, as far as Ash could tell.

"You have confused the matter, I am afraid, Miss Winter," he told her calmly, forcing a polite smile. "Seducing you is not my aim at all. Rather, I am aiding my brother in his search for a bride."

She appeared distinctly unimpressed. "While offering His Grace your assistance is commendable, I fear you are wasting your time with me. I have no intention of marrying."

No intention of marrying?

Just what manner of female *was* Miss Prudence Winter?

Want more? Look for Ash and Pru's story, *Wagered in Winter*, here!

Don't miss Scarlett's other romances!

(Listed by Series)

Complete Book List
scarlettscottauthor.com/books

HISTORICAL ROMANCE

Heart's Temptation
A Mad Passion (Book One)
Rebel Love (Book Two)
Reckless Need (Book Three)
Sweet Scandal (Book Four)
Restless Rake (Book Five)
Darling Duke (Book Six)
The Night Before Scandal (Book Seven)

Wicked Husbands
Her Errant Earl (Book One)
Her Lovestruck Lord (Book Two)
Her Reformed Rake (Book Three)
Her Deceptive Duke (Book Four)
Her Missing Marquess (Book Five)

League of Dukes
Nobody's Duke (Book One)
Heartless Duke (Book Two)
Dangerous Duke (Book Three)
Shameless Duke (Book Four)
Scandalous Duke (Book Five)

Sins and Scoundrels
Duke of Depravity (Book One)
Prince of Persuasion (Book Two)
Marquess of Mayhem (Book Three)
Earl of Every Sin (Book Four)

The Wicked Winters
Wicked in Winter (Book One)
Wedded in Winter (Book Two) ~ Available in the special, limited edition box set *Once Upon A Christmas Wedding*
Wanton in Winter (Book Three)
Wishes in Winter (Book 3.5) ~ Available in *A Lady's Christmas Rake*
Willful in Winter (Book Four)
Wagered in Winter (Book Five)
Wild in Winter (Book Six)
Wooed in Winter (Book Seven) ~ Available in *Lords, Ladies and Babies*

Stand-alone Novella
Lord of Pirates

CONTEMPORARY ROMANCE

Love's Second Chance
Reprieve (Book One)
Perfect Persuasion (Book Two)
Win My Love (Book Three)

Coastal Heat
Loved Up (Book One)

About the Author

USA Today and Amazon bestselling author Scarlett Scott writes steamy Victorian and Regency romance with strong, intelligent heroines and sexy alpha heroes. She lives in Pennsylvania with her Canadian husband, adorable identical twins, and one TV-loving dog.

A self-professed literary junkie and nerd, she loves reading anything, but especially romance novels, poetry, and Middle English verse. Catch up with her on her website www.scarlettscottauthor.com. Hearing from readers never fails to make her day.

Scarlett's complete book list and information about upcoming releases can be found at www.scarlettscottauthor.com.

Connect with Scarlett! You can find her here:
Join Scarlett Scott's reader's group on Facebook for early excerpts, giveaways, and a whole lot of fun!
Sign up for her newsletter here.
scarlettscottauthor.com/contact
Follow Scarlett on Amazon
Follow Scarlett on BookBub
www.instagram.com/scarlettscottauthor
www.twitter.com/scarscoromance
www.pinterest.com/scarlettscott
www.facebook.com/AuthorScarlettScott
Join the Historical Harlots on Facebook

Made in the USA
Monee, IL
13 April 2020